Ju
F
Sch 3 Schloss, Ezekiel, comp.
The new World over
story book.

Temple Israel Library
Minneapolis, Minn.

Please sign your full name on the above card.

Return books promptly to the Library or Temple Office.

Fines will be charged for overdue books or for damage or loss of same.

The New
World Over
STORY BOOK

From the pages of World Over Magazine

Published by the

Jewish Education Committee of New York

The New World Over
STORY BOOK

An Illustrated Anthology

for Jewish Youth

EDITED BY

EZEKIEL SCHLOSS AND MORRIS EPSTEIN

Bloch Publishing Company · New York

Library of Congress Catalog Card Number: 67-26645

Contents

I. IN THE JEWISH STATE

II. THE WORLD OF EASTERN EUROPE

III. THE BIBLE AS BACKGROUND

Introduction

FIFTEEN YEARS have sped by since I wrote the introduction to the first WORLD OVER STORY BOOK. I had not long stood at the helm of the JEC then, but long enough to know, and to say, that WORLD OVER's appeal was universal and that it was the "darling of the JEC." The magazine, with a circulation of 40,000, was entering its second decade, and I thought it reasonable and prudent to pray that it attain Bar Mitzvah age in health and accomplishment.

As I look back on my tenure as executive vice president, a role which has now passed to a distinguished colleague, I can truthfully say that few JEC endeavors have brought me as much joy and as great a sense of fulfillment as has WORLD OVER.

The knowledge that every second Friday during the school year we were shipping to 100,000 subscribers—for thus had the list prospered—a magazine that strove in every line of text and illustration to make the Jewish tradition and heritage meaningful and pleasurable to our Jewish youth was a continuous source of joy. To realize that every issue, from sparkling cover to captivating back page, conveyed literature, fine art, timely news, first-hand glimpses of Jewish communities here, in Israel, and in other lands of Jewish settlement, was an endless fount of inspiration.

The constant stream of commendatory letters that came from children—many of them in that group that was with loving care being taught to remember what their parents had unfortunately tried to forget—was balm that salved the irritations and frustrations of daily chores.

Encouragement came as well from parents and educators. The former saw in WORLD OVER a home and family magazine, unlike any produced in the United States or elsewhere, for that matter. It could buttress Jewish family life and observance and it bridged the gap between school and home. The latter discerned in WORLD OVER a trusty tool, a friend that enlivened formal instruction in Bible, holidays, history, and Jewish ways of life. And in WORLD OVER's special issues, everyone found pulsating texts, fresh with unhackneyed material, instinct with a point of view.

Not the least of my gratifications derived from the widespread acceptance of WORLD OVER. Has there ever been a Jewish periodical boasting such a genuine K'lal Yisrael outlook, a publication so unremittingly an exponent of normative Judaism yet so warmly welcome in Jewish classrooms and homes of every ideological shade? I cannot think of any, and I have been active in Jewish public affairs for almost fifty years.

For over a quarter of a century, then, WORLD OVER has been zealously pursuing its mission—to be a magazine that helps Jewish children grow into responsible citizens solidly aware of the values inherent in their rich Jewish heritage. With every story-telling picture, with every page of fiction, classical and new, with every timely and topical feature, indeed with every puzzle and cartoon, the magazine portrays Jewish life, past and present. Moreover—and this is a special point of pride—WORLD OVER has served not only New York, the primary beneficiary of the JEC's program, but the American Jewish community, and world Jewry as well.

And now the time has come to dip into the vast resources that have accumulated since the last Story Book. Before you is spread the feast of a second anthology. One day there will be a third, and why not a fourth? For WORLD OVER has become nothing less than an institution in contemporary Jewish life, and our prayer in this volume is that it may reach its golden anniversary with the grace and youthful vigor that are so uniquely its own.

As JEC director I basked in WORLD OVER's reputation, but I was ultimately answerable for its content and appearance. Fortunately, this responsibility never became a burden, for during all these years the day-to-day destiny of the magazine was—and continues to be—in the capable hands of men whose names have come to be synonymous with WORLD OVER itself, Ezekiel Schloss and Morris Epstein.

Mr. Schloss has conferred upon WORLD OVER an artistic distinction unmatched in American Jewish juvenile periodicals. His covers and his art direction testify to a prodigal fecundity and constitute a veritable gallery of festival, biblical, and historical illustration and portraiture.

Dr. Epstein has brought to WORLD OVER a prolific pen, a keen respect for the written word, an abhorrence of the shoddy, a happy ability to cultivate a world-wide roster of authors whom he has befriended, and a thorough training in Jewish and secular disciplines.

Together, these veterans have infused WORLD OVER with Jewish spirit and journalistic strength. They have, in a word, made WORLD OVER what it is today.

I wish also to acknowledge with deep appreciation the work of associate art director Sigmund Laufer, whose dedicated labor is evident in the aesthetic physical appearance of each issue of the magazine.

Finally, it is with sincere pleasure that I pay tribute to a grand lady, Miss Gertrude Weil, of Goldsboro, N.C., whose warm-hearted generosity has made possible the publication of this volume.

To all of you, dear friends, and to the generation of children who have been and who will yet be WORLD OVER's staunchest supporters, may this volume in days to come communicate to you the glow and the satisfaction with which I write these words now.

AZRIEL EISENBERG

I

In the Jewish State

Poor Afura

BY JACK HOROWITZ

IT WAS visiting day in Kfar Yarok, "The Green Village." Shlomo, the director, felt a warm glow as his eyes scanned the fields and buildings of the children's village of the Youth Aliyah. Shlomo was proud of the children who had come to the settlement from far-off places like Romania, Persia, Yugoslavia, Iraq, Poland, Hong Kong, India, and Chile. When these boys and girls had first arrived, they were strangers, used to different ways of life, different foods, different dress. They did not even have a common language. Now they were members of one community.

Shlomo watched Yaffa, busy at work. She was a pretty orphan girl from Poland, whose father and mother had been killed by the Nazis. Yaffa's big brown eyes were always sad. How frightened she was when she first arrived at Kfar Yarok! During the meals, Yaffa would sneak pieces of bread into her pockets, and hide them under her pillow. Many weeks passed before she came to understand that she was no longer living like a hunted animal in the forests of Poland.

The other children had been kind and patient. Slowly, the terrible fear left her eyes, and she came to trust and love her friends. Now she managed the dining hall, and smiled proudly when the boys and girls came in for their meals.

Shlomo looked towards the chicken house and heard Amnon, singing to himself. Soon Amnon appeared, carrying a basket of eggs. He was a strong, sturdy lad, with black curly hair. "How different he is now!" Shlomo thought.

Amnon had come from Iraq. His parents had settled in the wastelands of the Negev. They had sent Amnon to the children's village to learn Hebrew and farming in the mod-

3

ern village school.

At first Amnon spoke only Arabic. He took to farm life quickly. But Shlomo shivered at the memory of the first month of Amnon's arrival in the village. He had carried a knife in his pocket. One afternoon, the boys were playing dodge-ball. Amnon stood silently, watching. Suddenly Moshe, a lanky youngster, seized the ball and, throwing it directly at Amnon, shouted:

"Here, boy. Come and play too."

Amnon tried to dodge the ball but it was too late. It hit him on the side of the head. No one was prepared for what followed next. In a flash Amnon whipped his knife out, and flipped the sharp, curved blade open. With a snarl he crouched over and moved towards Moshe. Moshe stood shocked, frozen to the ground. Shlomo had quickly jumped between the boys. He looked steadily at Amnon and said in Arabic, "Amnon, here in Israel we don't fight one another. We are all friends. Moshe meant no harm. He is on *your* side."

Slowly the wild anger left Amnon's eyes. He lowered the knife and his anger turned to shame. Turning, he fled to his room. Shlomo found him there, lying on his bed sobbing bitterly. They had a good heart-to-heart talk. Amnon told Shlomo of the cruel knife-battles he was forced to fight in Iraq. It was dangerous to go without the protection of a knife against the Arab teen-age gangs who roamed the market places. Amnon, too, had slowly learned to trust the other boys, and became part of the young community at Kfar Yarok.

Shlomo was awakened from his daydream by the shouts of the children. "They're here! They're here!" From every direction of the village the boys and girls ran to the roadway, where a bus had just arrived. Parents, relatives and friends

poured out of the bus. Shlomo's brother Yoel, a colonel in the Israel Defense Army, stepped out.

"*Shalom Aleikhem,* Shlomo," he said. "You are doing a grand job. You couldn't find a healthier, happier, rosier bunch of youngsters anywhere."

That night, the children put on a program in the dining hall. A little redfaced boy stepped onto the platform and

Illustrated by Arie Haas

rang a bell. The chattering stopped as he spoke:

"*Haverim* and *Haverot,* ladies and gentlemen. It delights me to present our program. You will hear our choir, and see the products of our farm. But first we will hear from Barukh, who has a very important message for you."

Barukh, thin and lanky, looked directly at Shlomo. He smiled and began to read from a notebook.

"This is supposed to be a good place. They say it is a model village." He read slowly, punctuating each pause with a quick glance around.

"I don't think so. The Bible says 'Seek justice, relieve the oppressed, protect the fatherless.' But there is only injustice here!"

Shlomo was shocked. Guests looked at one another, surprised and bewildered.

"I want to tell you about one of our girls and you'll see for yourself. I met her in the gardens. She worked hard, and never complained. She never talked about herself, and that's why I'm doing the talking for her. It's time something was done."

He continued: "Listen to the injustices she has suffered. First they gave her the roughest chores, because they knew she wouldn't complain. She was really sick once, and Geulah wouldn't even come to her."

Geulah, the village nurse, blushed as all the startled eyes turned to her.

"She lives in a broken-down room. The roof is always leaking but she never grumbles. No one invites her to any parties. She just stands in her room, lonely and sad. In fact, she isn't even here right now, but alone in her room."

A buzz began to fill the hall, but Barukh seemed not to notice it. "She always has stomach trouble," he said. "I tried to talk to Yaffa about it, she just laughed at me."

Yaffa trembled. An embarrassed and bewildered look spread over her face. Shlomo began to rise to his feet in anger, but Yoel grabbed his wrist. "We're going to get to the bottom of this," he said through clenched teeth. "Let him finish."

"Yes, it's really bad," Barukh continued. "Now we appeal to you to do something about the situation. Shlomo won't help her."

Poor Shlomo winced. A triumphant look darted across Barukh's flushed face.

"And you all know whom I'm talking about." There was a dreadful silence in the room. "It's Afura! That's who it is, Afura!"

The tense room exploded into laughter and cheers. Shlomo doubled over in laughter. Yoel was completely confused. "Has everyone gone mad?" He shouted.

There were tears in Shlomo's eyes, tears of great laughter, when he turned to Yoel. "Don't you understand? Afura is our old gray mare. Her stable is in the corner of the barn."

After the evening program was over, the whole audience joined in a lively hora. The words of the song that accompanied the dance carried a special meaning for Shlomo that night:

"Our strength is our faith. Together we shall rebuild Israel. Arise, O brethren, and come. Zion awaits you."

As the circle went around, Shlomo thought to himself: "They are now one people, my youngsters, and they will make good builders, good citizens of Israel, and good human beings."

Cave of Adventure

BY AZRIEL EISENBERG

"ALLAH help me find that goat!" The young Arab boy lifted his eyes in prayer to the god of his Moslem ancestors. "If I return without it, the sheik will surely beat me. My back will be sore for days and I, Mohammed the Wolf, will be shamed before the whole Ta-amirah tribe!"

Drenched with sweat from his exertions, young Mohammed peered about him for the lost goat. In the distance he saw the shimmering waters of the Dead Sea. Its strong salty odor did not bother him, for he was accustomed to the smell, having often visited this part of Palestine, the ancient Holy Land, with the wandering tribe of Bedouin smugglers to which he belonged.

Nearby was the spring of Ain Feshkha, the only fresh water to be found on the high plateau. So that they would not die of thirst, the tribe had chosen this particular camping place as they traveled from the Kingdom of Jordan to the city of Bethlehem in Palestine with their smuggled goats and other goods.

Round about Mohammed lay the dry and uninhabited Wadi Qumran, a barren wasteland bordering the Dead Sea. The waving grass, burned yellow by the sun, was the only growing thing on the hills above the Dead Sea, which is really a large salt lake far below sea level. The surrounding rocks and caves have given temporary shelter to soldiers, hermits, holy men, and outlaws, since biblical times. But nobody has made his home there for hundreds of years.

"Curses on that goat!" Mohammed rasped from his dry throat. "The tribe wants to get on to Bethlehem and he's holding us back. I'll die in this heat before I ever find him!"

Mohammed was about to give up his fruitless search for the lost goat when he suddenly came upon the entrance to a cave he had not seen before.

"Ah!" he exclaimed in relief, "that cursed goat has probably wandered in there!"

The cave was dark and silent, and Mohammed was frightened as he tried to see inside. He picked up a stone and cautiously tossed it into the opening. He hoped to hear the bleating of his goat, but instead a sharp crash broke the stillness of the desert.

Scared by the unexpected noise, "the Wolf" jumped in fright and, turning tail, raced back to the ragged black tents

Illustrated by William Sayles

of the Ta-amirah.

The elders of the tribe were resting during the midday heat, while their mustard-colored camels quietly grazed outside. In that year of 1947, the more prosperous Arabs rode in modern automobiles. But the poorer Bedouin kept to the old and time-honored mode of desert transportation, the camel.

Mohammed threw himself down on the ground, his heart beating wildly. Later, when he had recovered both breath and courage, he called softly to his younger friend, Musa. A dark face appeared around the flap of a tent, and Mohammed beckoned with his hand.

"Musa," he whispered hoarsely. "I think I've found something strange in a cave!"

The two boys joined hands and raced back to the cave. The entrance was partly obstructed by rocks, leaving only a small opening. "You stand guard, Musa," said Mohammed.

Mohammed tossed off his burnoose and crawled through the opening. He moved on hands and knees for several feet through a narrow passage which turned slightly downward. At last Mohammed found himself in a shadowy room. It was about six feet wide and a little higher than that, so he was able to stand up.

Crumbling jars lined the walls. Among the broken pieces he could see decaying cloth-wrapped objects that looked like little packages.

Carefully tiptoeing over to an unbroken jug, Mohammed cautiously lifted the circular lid. A horrible stench choked his nostrils and made him cough. Putting a hand down into the jar, he pulled out a dusty bundle of cloth . . . then another . . . and still another.

Mohammed carefully crept back out of the cave. He placed the bundles on the ground outside, and Musa stared

at the curious find.

"What in heaven's name can they be?" he exclaimed.

Carefully Mohammed peeled the cloth from a bundle. The cover appeared to be linen, which seemed to be coated with either pitch or wax. Underneath were rolled-up sheets, apparently made from sheepskin or some other leather. They were sewn together and marked with strange writing.

"Maybe," Musa wondered, "they tell where there is some buried treasure!"

"Yes." Mohammed nodded his head. "Or perhaps explain how to perform some kind of magic!"

"Well, what shall we do with them, O wise one?" Musa mocked his good friend.

"We will take them to the chief of our tribe," Mohammed replied thoughtfully. "The sheik will know what to do. When we get to the market place in Bethlehem, there may be someone there who understands the language they are written in. And perhaps he will offer us a good price for them."

"Yes," Musa nodded in agreement. "They might be worth a lot of money, and we'll all be rich. My grandfather is always telling about the crazy strangers from foreign lands who come here and dig up old things to take to their own countries."

"You're right," replied Mohammed, patting his friend approvingly. "They go to the trouble of digging up old cities like Tell-el-Mutesellim, where they find pottery jugs and other things. By the way, Musa: how about the jars in the cave? We can always use them for carrying water, even if they have no other value. Let's get the one these rolls came in."

The two boys crawled back into the cave together. Carrying out the empty clay jar, they replaced its contents. Then between them they lugged their heavy discovery to camp, resting frequently on the way.

"Say, Mohammed," Musa reminded his companion at one stop, "you never found that goat!"

"Maybe the sheik will forgive me," Mohammed said thoughtfully, "when we show him what's in this old jug."

"I wouldn't be surprised," Musa said, "if what we've got is worth more than a goat. Even more than a camel, or a horse!"

In the excitement of the occasion, Mohammed fell in with Musa's dream of wealth. "Perhaps the sheik won't punish me at all. I'll bet he'll give me a present," Mohammed said wistfully, and generously added, "If he does, I'll share it with you, Musa, because you helped me and are my very good friend."

Picking up the jar, off they went again, in a rush, eager to show the strange find to their chief. Soon they would know whether Mohammed would be punished or rewarded for the day's adventure.

That Wonderful Jackknife

BY WILLIAM JACOB

SAADIA saw the beautiful jackknife at Lod Airport near Tel Aviv that bright morning when the great Hebrew eagle of a plane had sped them in a blink of a goat's eye from Yemen.

Then came the bus ride from Lod to the temporary camp for new immigrants, the *Ma'abarah,* which their white-bearded rabbi had mentioned when, like the Prophet Ezra, he explained:

"And no more the unloved residents of a bitter nation where the Torah is forbidden. With Jewish brothers from each corner of the world, you will learn to work, to make holy the soil of your ancestors, and enjoy the fruit of your labor."

From the bus he watched the rolling chessboard of the Holy Land, and wondered at the strange constructions and monster-like machines, things for which he had yet to find the names. And glowing behind it all was the wonderful jackknife; it somehow stood for all those nameless marvels making him dizzy in his sun-scorched, shepherd's head.

From the moment the bus pulled into the neat rows of houses with green garden porches, the never-ending lesson of a new world to learn had begun. Even now that he was a veteran of three months in Israel, he puzzled at how, in twelve full years of his life in Yemen, he'd known so little of this world. That, for example, the Hebrew word *tzarif,* for "shack," defined the cozy wooden home just for them, for his mother and three sisters and himself. And an invention like the fine little shed out in back, shared by his family and the one next door, that sheltered the fascinating "miracle of the chain"—just one good pull and mad torrents of clear water gushed and swirled in the pearl-like well.

And now he was a gardener: a real man's job even before his Bar Mitzvah.

With the sun smiling hot on his back, Saadia sat pulling weeds in their garden in front of the house. With all of his new wisdom he was thinking hard about his great discovery and . . . the *plan* he'd awakened with this morning. But just then his mother's voice broke into his thoughts, singing out from her chores in the house:

"Saadia. Don't forget again to get new work pants from the main office. I want to fix those rags you seem to like so well."

He didn't pay much attention, for he was a little angry. He yanked at another weed, thinking of how he had run to his mother like a simple child, with the news of his discovery. Exploring the *Ma'abarah* with his good friend, he had come upon the General Store. It was just a plain cement-block building. Ah, but *inside!* He was sure that in all of Yemen there was not a bazaar that contained such a dazzling array of treasure. There were fine metal clocks each with a bell inside, to wake you up in the morning, the man said; and all kinds of tools that would make any task easier. And *there,* for all to see in a case on the counter, was the perfect twin to the wonderful Israeli jackknife.

The huge, red-haired storekeeper had smilingly pushed the case toward him. And Saadia felt his eyes open wide on that five bladed masterpiece as the storekeeper, like the genie of the three wishes, unfolded the beautiful bright steel from its polished bone handle. There was a blade for cutting

anything; then a smaller one; an awl for leather; a cork-screw; and a tiny pair of scissors.

"That's a product of Israel, a genuine scout knife, and its price is eight pounds [almost $3]," the smiling store-keeper said.

Then Saadia explained to his mother the importance, the necessity of owning that knife. It would change him instant-ly into a real Israeli; a boy of the modern world. But, alas, his mother was a woman and could not understand the dreams of a man.

"But tomorrow morning my plan shall begin," he de-cided. "Tomorrow I shall have the money."

That afternoon he sat quietly in the schoolroom, but his thoughts did not. And later, in bed, he heard the entire symphony of the sounds of the night, till the morning birds told him it was *time* . . .

Illustrated by Uri Shulevitz

Then he ran to the road and the bus stop with his piasters, his coins, clasped in his hand. He bought a ticket to get him there and back, from the Place of Orange Groves. Then he pushed on the seat in front to help the bus get there in time.

Arriving, he met a few boys his own age, but most were older, and all waiting to work at picking the oranges. In Hebrew he shouted to the hiring man, "I'm strong as a camel and a real gardener as well," and he was taken with the others to work in the groves.

In no time at all he was able to pick the sweet-smelling oranges and place them in brown cartons, as though he had done nothing else all his life. And when the job was done, four crisp blue Israeli pound notes were pressed into his hand.

He was removing the return ticket from inside his cap while waiting in line to board one of the three buses, when suddenly—he just barely seemed to see from the corner of his eye a faint bit of blue fluttering lightly upon the ground. Refusing to think of what he thought he saw, he looked up instead, gazing at the distant green hills.

The first two buses filled and rolled away. The few remaining boys were climbing into the last bus. He bent quickly to the ground and scooped up the stiff, folded blue paper and it tingled in his hand. Then he ran to catch up with the others.

With a seat to himself in the back he examined his find. A guilty swallow strained past his throat as, for the second time, he counted four clean Israeli pound notes. *And some poor boy had lost them.* But, he told himself, the boy must be gone in another bus; and he jammed the notes into his pocket, adding contentedly: four plus four equals the price of the knife.

Stepping down at the Ma'abarah he fairly flew to his house and to the corner of the room that was his own. He plunged his hand into his pocket and found . . . Nothing! Only the empty holes and rips of his short khaki work pants. Then suddenly he knew! The four pounds he had found *were his own.* And now they were gone forever.

He swallowed hard, pushed a smile onto his face, and thought:

"What does it matter? I left home without money and returned in no way worse. I have become an expert picker of oranges and have traveled alone in the Holy Land. And . . . I thought to keep that which was not mine, that I thought another had lost, and I suffered the same loss. But I have gained. I am wiser."

His mother startled him then as she came into the room. "Saadia . . . I've had Amos looking for you everywhere. The crop of what you and your gardening have grown has been sold. Now you are an Israeli in truth. So come take the knife you have earned."

Adventure in the Forest

BY YEMIMA TCHERNOWITZ

I'VE BEEN WONDERING how to begin my story, and at last I've come to a wonderful decision: the best place to start is at the beginning!

First, you'll have to imagine yourself inside Israel. It's easy; just close your eyes and—Whoosh! Wasn't that a quick trip? Now come along to Kibbutz May M'nuhot (which in Hebrew means "still waters") .

A kibbutz, you know, is where people live like one big

family. The land is leased from the Jewish National Fund, and no hired help work there. It's share and share alike, some working in the fields, some in the gardens, in the barns, in the machine shops.

And what a life for the kids! When they're born, they are taken to an infant house. At the age of two, they are transferred to a nursery. Later, they go to school until they are ready to join fellow workers in the kibbutz.

And now, back to Kibbutz May M'nuhot where I want you to meet our heroes, Udi and Nir. Who are they, you ask? Well, just mention those names to anyone in the kibbutz, that's all. Everybody knows Udi and Nir, the "Siamese twins." They go together like bread and butter. They were born on the same day, at the same hour, and have been inseparable since. Are they brothers? No. They're not even related, as you can see by just looking at them.

Udi is brown as coffee beans, from his head to the soles of his feet, which are always muddy, even when it's not raining. Nir is a redhead and so freckled that his friends say he must have been sunburned while lying in a net!

They're not in the same class, either. Udi is in the first grade, Nir in the second. And their parents live at opposite ends of the kibbutz. Now—why are they known as the "Siamese twins?"

Because they are both collectors. They collect everything. Empty their pockets and you'll find a museum. Hairs of a horse's tail, large stones, small stones, old bottle tops. One day, it is said, a porcupine hopped out of Udi's pocket. Did everybody run! And another time two green frogs leaped from Nir's pants and croaked their way to the teacher's desk. That ended classes for the day! All the children in the kibbutz have caught "collector's fever" from this pair at one time or another. Stamps, candy wrappers, silver foil—

there was simply no end of it.

Another thing that sets Udi and Nir apart is their "secret-izing." After all, the kibbutz children are all brought up together. They play together and study together. Why shouldn't they share secrets? They do, except Udi and Nir. What usually happens is that one child has a secret; he tells the secret to his friend; the friend tells it to another friend; and soon enough, everyone in the kibbutz is in on "the secret." But not Udi and Nir. They never reveal their secrets. It goes like this: Udi says, "Nir, I've got something to tell you. Come here." And then, "Bz-zz, b-zz, b-z-z." And another secret is born. No wonder everyone is jealous of that pair!

As if that isn't enough, Udi and Nir have a hiding place. When they were practically infants—one in nursery school,

Illustrated by Gabe Josephson

the other in kindergarten—they used to hide under the table, you know, where the tablecloth almost touches the floor and makes a kind of hiding place. There the two would sit, hiding, and they kept hiding, here, there, and everywhere, even when they were twelve and thirteen years old. It finally turned into a sort of detective game. Everyone would try to find the hiding place. All the kids became sleuths, trailing the "secretizers," till one would suddenly cry out:

"Here it is!"

And there would be a scramble of voices: "Here is what? What did you find?"

The reply would be the same each time: "The hiding place of the Siamese twins!"

And then the detective who had uncovered the lair would proudly lead all the kids to his discovery. There they found Udi and Nir, sitting and emptying their pockets, pockets full of treasure. Sometimes, the hiding place was in the silo, full of grain, sometimes in back of the chicken coop, sometimes in a corner in the stable, and sometimes in the watchman's hut, in the vineyard.

If that was all I had to tell about Udi and Nir, there wouldn't be any story. But one day, this strange pair pushed matters to the limit and the whole kibbutz was in an uproar as a result.

Not far from the Kibbutz May M'nuhot there is a thick forest. It was planted here by the first halutzim, the early pioneers of Israel. In the winter, the trees rustle pleasantly with the blowing, and when there is a storm, whistling noises send shivers down your spine.

But in summer, the forest gives shelter to the weary and is a pleasant host to the children who play in the branches. Inside the forest, however, real danger lies wait-

ing for the unwary. Once a leopard was caught in there, and next day a dead rabbit was found in the leopard's tracks. There are some who say that on cold winter nights, a black she-wolf stalks in search of prey and her howling is fearful to hear. In short, everything you ever heard about forests and their dangers is told as well about the forest near Kibbutz May M'nuhot . . .

Even . . . robbers! Yes, they once caught a band of armed bandits in the thick of the forest. They had planned to sneak into the kibbutz and steal a cow or a horse or a mule from the stable. Luckily, they were foiled. No wonder, then, that small children skirt the forest carefully when they are out on a picnic. And at night, everybody keeps his distance. But Udi and Nir, were they afraid of the forest? Why drag out the suspense? I might as well get started immediately with the thrilling tale I have to unfold. No one knows where the rumor about the discovery started. But it spread like wildfire in the dining room, from mouth to mouth, until the place was a-quiver with the news. It all centered about the fact that excavations had been made by the Department of Antiquities of Israel, and that in these excavations there had been uncovered the floor of an ancient synagogue. It dated back to the time of the Hasmoneans.

We're always digging up fascinating things in Israel, because our land is so old and because the Jewish people lived there for so long. But all the way back to the time of Judah Maccabee—that was super-unusual.

As everyone was gossiping about the new find, a report filtered into the dining room. Udi and Nir were "secretizing" out on the porch. The next day, the mystery deepened. Because Udi and Nir had disappeared. Everybody joined in the search. They looked in the stable, in the chicken-coop, even near the brook. It was as if the earth had swallowed them up.

At last, someone thought of going to the apartment of Udi's parents, who happened to be in the city that day. Ethan, the boy who was leading the search, cried out: "Look! A note on the table!"

Quickly he opened it and read it aloud: "Two Hasmoneans without any fear. Udi is one, the other is Nir. Our address: The Hill of Aytey."

There was an uproar. Everybody wanted to tell the police to call out the army, to turn the whole neighborhood upside down. But Ethan put a stop to all that nonsense. He had an idea, he said, and everyone gathered around to listen. What a lot of head-nodding and buzzing there was. I wish I could tell you about it right now, but meanwhile . .

Let's go back to the forest. It was almost sunset and the sun filled the sky with all colors of the rainbow. The green leaves on the trees suddenly changed to an eerie shade of rose and gray. And in the heart of the forest were only two lonely, wandering souls—Udi and Nir.

*   *   *

Uproar in the kibbutz; silence in the forest. And all because Udi and Nir, brave adventurers, were now in the heart of the dark and awesome forest not far from the kibbutz.

Did I say "brave?" You might accuse me of exaggeration if you were to come on Udi and Nir at that moment. The sun was about to set. In Israel, twilight comes and goes very quickly. The forest was already alive with eerie shadows. Under a tall cypress tree, a little boy turned with a solemn expression to his freckle-faced friend.

"Nir, do you think we ought to go back?"

"Back w-where?"

"To the kibbutz, of course. It's still a long way to the Hill of Aytey."

Nir seemed to draw courage from Udi's hesitation and he said, staunchly, "Don't be a droop. That stone we found —I want to see if it fits the floor of the you-know-what." (Even when they were alone, they seemed to "secretize," they were so used to it!) "And besides—"

"But, look," Udi pleaded. "It's practically dark and if we go back now, we'll just be in time for dinner . . ."

"Say, is that all you can think of—dinner?" Nir was indignant. "We've got more important things to think about at a time like this! You heard what the older *haverim* said. The hill is at the end of the forest, not far from the path. A few more steps, and we'll be there. I'll tell you what. Give me your hand and we will go faster."

Udi silently slid his hand into Nir's and again the two started to walk.

If you hold a friend's hand, the danger seems to lessen. Udi felt that the hand of Nir suddenly became big and strong.

At once the darkness fell on the forest. As if it had been hidden behind one of the trees, had peeked and seen the sunset, and announced: "Here I am!" In the darkness it is pleasant sometimes to be in bed when mother is nearby or

when the night watch-lady goes about in the kibbutz and you hear the breath of sleeping children alongside yourself; but in the forest, the darkness is so dark! Then the trees take on quite frightening shapes. One is a giant, stretching forth his arms; another is a dwarf waiting to trip you up, a third is a witch with leafy hands reaching out to grab you!

"Nir, are we going in the right direction?"

"Of course, our direction is due west!"

"But how do you know which way west is?"

"Don't you learn anything in school?" Nir said scornfully. "West is where the sun sets."

"But the sun has already set, so how can you tell?"

"We have a compass!"

"But you know that our compass is a toy! We only use

it to show off with in front of the kids!"

By now Nir began to be convinced. He paused and scowled, and took another few steps, and then, all at once, the Hill of Aytey loomed before their eyes.

They started to climb quickly, as if the hill could walk and would run away.

CR-A-SH! They came flying down.

"Help!" yelled Udi, because he was younger.

"Help!" yelled Nir, because he was older.

Down they rolled, like two balls, and the miracle was that they weren't badly hurt. ("God watches over fools," says the Bible—even small fools, like Udi and Nir, you might add!)

"Nir, are you alive?"

"I don't know, are you?"

"I think so, but my foot hurts."

"You're bleeding! Wait, I'll tie it with my handkerchief." Nir stuck his hand into his pocket. He dug deeper and deeper in that cavern of a pocket, stooping lower and lower, when suddenly his eye caught sight of something and he fell to the ground, forgetting the handkerchief, Udi, everything.

Because there, under a clod of earth, he beheld a sight that would surely bring joy and pride into the heart of every member of Kibbutz May M'nuhot. It was a small clay pitcher and on it . . .

"A coin! Engraved on the pitcher! I see it by the light of the stars! It must be—it is—from the time of Hasmoneans!"

Nir's voice sounded the way **Columbus'** must have when he discovered America, or Edison's when he invented the electric light—like the voice of all the great discoverers. But Udi sat quietly, and held his foot in his hand, and his foot hurt. And when a foot hurts a child who is a first-grader in

school, then even a pitcher from the time of the Maccabees, even with a coin engraved upon it, does not make that
foot feel any better.

Nir came closer, to show Udi the pitcher, when, without
warning, something swished through the air. Suddenly Udi
and Nir were surrounded by figures draped in white.

"RETURN MY PITCHER!" said a deep voice.

"But we f-found it," Nir stammered bravely. "W-Who
are you?"

"He is Judah Maccabee!" came another voice. Strangely,
it sounded like Ruthie, a girl in the kibbutz, but what was
she doing with Judah Maccabee?

"Why have you come here in the dark of the night?" said
the mysterious voice. "Why do you disturb my kingdom?
And why do you 'secretize' in the kibbutz? Why are you
always hiding from the other kids?"

That did it. Judah Maccabee wouldn't use a word like
"kids"! Nir pointed at the white-clad figure. "You're not
Judah Maccabee. You are . . . "

He got no further. Strong arms grabbed Udi and Nir,
trussed them up, blindfolded them, while other voices
cried: "Off with them! Into captivity with the enemy!"

Above the shouting, Nir cried, "Don't be afraid, Udi!
I've got the pitcher. I know who . . ."

Udi heard no more. He was in a blanket, and it was
warm and pleasant, and his foot didn't hurt any more, and
the last thing he heard was laughter, laughter all around
him . . .

When he awoke, it was morning. He was lying in his bed,
and Sarah, the kibbutz nurse, raised the shade and said as
usual, "Good morning, Udi, time to get up."

Udi moved and felt a sharp pain in his leg. Sarah said,
"Udi, where did you get this bruise?"

Udi said simply, "From Judah Maccabee." Sarah thought the boy was still dreaming. She tiptoed out and softly closed the door. Udi fell asieep again.

Next day, Udi felt better. He hobbled outside and saw Nir. "Come on," said Nir. "We've been called to appear before the administration of the kibbutz. They came this morning and took the pitcher away."

Udi nodded. So the pitcher was real. It wasn't a dream. He felt better. All the kids gaped at Udi and Nir as the pair was excused from school and marched to the administration office.

On a table stood the pitcher—their pitcher. And every-body looked excited. Gideon, the executive secretary, spoke.

"*Haverim,*" he said, "the pitcher which you found is very ancient, and we have to notify the Department of Antiquities of the Government. Meanwhile we will hold it for safety. Congratulations, *Haverim!*"

The Government solved the riddle of the pitcher, but Udi and Nir never solved the mystery of the strangers in the forest. And yet, a curious thing happened. From that adventure-filled night on, Udi and Nir were no longer "Siamese twins." They never discussed it, you understand, but they stopped whispering to each other and hiding and keeping secrets from their friends. They were too grownup, too important for such baby stuff.

And their pockets? Practically empty. Who could keep a rusty, spoiled compass, after finding a rare Hasmonean pitcher!

It just goes to show—you never know what will result from an adventure in the forest!

Of Donkeys, Detectives, and the Bible

BY FRIEDA CLARK HYMAN

EVERYONE loved Yeruham the Yemenite. Except, of course, robbers or smugglers. For Yeruham was a policeman; a detective, to be exact.

And Yeruham loved everyone. But most of all he loved the Bible. When Joel, his comrade, teased him, he would tap its cover and say, "It's all here, Joel, all."

"Everything?"

"Everything we have to know."

One day Yeruham was summoned to the office.

"The smugglers are busy again," the Captain said.

"Jews? Arabs?"

"Arabs, so it's up to you, Yeruham," the Captain said. "With your dark skin, you're the only one who can pass for an Arab."

"I'll do my best, sir." He saluted, and left.

A month later he was back. After whispering with Joel and the Captain, he said, "It's all set then. Tomorrow at ten."

"Yes, but remember," the Captain warned, "no matter what, you stay an Arab."

The next morning ten Arabs waited in a ravine near the Syrian border for a man called Ishmael. But one of them only *looked* like an Arab. Actually, he was Yeruham the Yemenite.

At 9:55 A.M., Ishmael arrived on a donkey. His sharp eyes counted the men. "All here. Good." He drew ten cotton pouches from his robe. "A quarter pound of heroin in each," he announced. "Sell the drug quickly."

Yeruham clenched his fist. Heroin! The terrible, habit-forming drug made from the bitter dried juice of the opium poppy. Heroin enslaved the minds of men, made them into useless human beings. This gang had to be stopped!

Yeruham's eyes darted from the heroin to the path that led into the ravine. It was ten o'clock. Where was Joel?

"Meet me in Haifa in a week," Ishmael commanded as he distributed the heroin. "In the same places. With the money. And remember, stay away from each other."

The men started for the path. "No!" Ishmael barked. "You have heroin on you. If you are discovered, it means the end. Keep off the roads. Across the hills."

As one man they vanished. Unwillingly, Yeruham did too.

But instead of continuing, he hid behind a clump of bushes. Almost immediately, he heard the car approaching.

Ishmael stiffened. The next second he slid off his donkey, and began climbing the rocks.

Yeruham bit his lips. If only he could seize Ishmael before he escaped! But he did not dare. Once he revealed his identity to any Arab, his usefulness was gone.

The auto screeched to a halt. Joel and four men rushed down the path. Yeruham waited, then slid into the ravine.

"Yeruham," Joel cried, "where are they?"

"There," he pointed above, "but it's too late."

"We had a flat tire," Joel exploded, "and now there's nothing but a donkey after all your work."

Yeruham pulled at his chin. "Hold on there, Joel," he said. "That donkey might still be able to tell us something."

"Of course," Joel mocked. "Why not? Balaam's donkey spoke. Come, little donkey," he snapped his fingers, "speak like your ancestor in the Bible did. Tell us who your master is." He paused. "No, you won't . . . or you can't?"

"JOEL!"

Joel flushed, ashamed. He had gone too far. One couldn't make fun of the Bible, and especially before Yeruham, who believed in its every word.

"I'm sorry, Yeruham. I just feel so rotten."

"Never mind. We *do* have the donkey. It will talk. I know it will."

Joel stared. "You are all right? The sun . . . ?"

"No, I'm not suffering from sunstroke. But the Bible does teach us if we know where to look."

"You don't really mean you believe this donkey can talk?"

"I believe in the truth of the Bible. In two days I'll prove this to you."

"With them, the Arabs?"

"No, back at the station. If it doesn't work, I'll return to them."

"But won't you have to report?"

"Not for another week. Now you take your men. I'll take the donkey."

The next two days were miserable ones for Yeruham and the donkey. For the donkey, because he had no food. For Yeruham, because he could not give him any. Finally the Captain came with Joel to see Yeruham.

"Joel tells me you expect the donkey to talk, Yeruham." the Captain said.

"In a manner of speaking, sir."

"Yeruham," the Captain said kindly, "you have been working too hard."

Instead of answering, Yeruham looked at his watch. "It's time, sir. You'll see."

He opened the barn. The donkey leaped out. Without hesitation it trotted away. Yeruham, the Captain and Joel followed. Into the Arab quarters up to a small villa he led

Illustrated by Gabe Josephson

them. Behind it they could see a barn.

The donkey brayed. The men ducked behind a tree. A door swung open. Ishmael appeared. Instantly Joel and the Captain flanked him. Joel stuck his hand into Ishmael's shirt and withdrew a bag of heroin.

As Ishmael was led away, Yeruham rushed to open the barn.

With a bound the donkey was inside. Ah, there it was. The stall, or "crib," with sweet, delicious hay. Eagerly the animal stuck its head into its goodness.

When Yeruham returned to the station, Joel and the Captain awaited him.

"Well?" they demanded. "Where is the passage in the Bible? We can't find it; and we searched high and low."

"Fine detectives!" Yeruham smiled.

"But there's nothing about a starving donkey. Balaam's wasn't even hungry."

"Then what about a donkey who knew his master's crib?"

"Oh," they gasped. "So that's it: 'The ox knoweth his owner, and the donkey his master's crib.' "

"So you do know." Yeruham's eyes twinkled.

"Isaiah," Joel said.

"Chapter 1, verse 3," the Captain added.

"Exactly. It's all there. All you have to know is where to look." And lovingly, Yeruham tapped his Bible.

Act of Faith

BY STELLA KAMP

THE PUPILS sat up in their seats. This was going to be a special lesson. For the rabbi himself was taking the class. Rabbi Stein smiled and said, *"Boker tov, talmidim."* The students replied happily.

Rabbi Stein's eyes twinkled behind his tortoise-rimmed glasses. *"Talmidim,* do you realize that we owe the privilege of studying the Torah to a man who lived about two thousand years ago? A brave man who risked his life to save the teachings of Judaism. Can anyone tell his name?"

Jonathan, the class showoff, immediately raised his hand. "Hillel," he answered.

The pupils grinned as the rabbi shook his head. "No, Jonathan. However, this man was a student of the great sage, Hillel. Today we are going to hear the dramatic story of Johanan ben Zakkai. But let us hear the story from the beginning. To do that, we must first turn back the pages of history to the year 66 of the Common Era."

Jerusalem had never been in such danger. In the Holy City, the determined patriots had overruled the peace party and encouraged the people to fight against the powerful Roman empire.

Nero, Emperor of Rome, realized that this was no temporary uprising of the Judeans; that this was a serious attempt to throw off the rule of Rome. He decided to send his most successful general, Vespasian, to Palestine. Vespasian would be just the man, he thought, to end this rebellion quickly.

This did not prove true. For two years, the Roman soldiers made no headway. The Judeans, with their home-forged weapons and their poorly trained soldiers, were steadily winning. As legion after legion of fresh soldiers were sent from Rome, they were defeated.

What Vespasian's troops could not do, the lack of strong leadership accomplished. The rebel leaders fought constantly among themselves. Then an enemy within the country entered the war. There were certain Judeans who, for a price, became informers, and sold the secrets of their own people to the enemy. The Romans began to win battles.

General Vespasian decided the time was ripe to strike hard. In his tent, he gave orders. "We will attack one city at a time and destroy it. The prize, Jerusalem, we will keep for the last. Then we will tear it down wall by wall with our battering rams."

So it was. One city after another fell before the Romans. When word came that Galilee was about to surrender, the people in the Holy City knew they were next and prepared for a fight to the finish.

Vespasian encircled Jerusalem with his army. He declared the city to be in a state of siege. No food was to be brought in. No one would be able to leave. The people in the Holy City were in a closed trap.

Inside the city was Johanan Ben Zakkai. He had sent for Joshua ben Hananya, one of his two devoted disciples, to come to him. Rabban Johanan ben Zakkai, one of the greatest teachers of Judaism since Hillel, thought of what was the best thing to do. His face was grim as he remembered how he had urged peace. The fiery patriots, known as the "zealots," would not listen. He had predicted defeat that terrible day. He knew the siege would starve the people into submission.

A knock roused him. It was Joshua. "Rabban Johanan," he said in his melodious voice, "you have sent for me. I came at once."

"Joshua, you must go into the city and bring my nephew, Ben Betiah, to me."

"Eliezer came with me. He felt he could be of more use to you here, Rabban Johanan."

Hearing his name, Eliezer ben Hyrkanos, the second of the rabbi's disciples, entered, carrying a scroll in his hand. Even now he was studying, ignoring the troubled times.

"There is much confusion in the city today, Rabban Johanan. They talk of nothing but the siege."

"That will make Joshua's task easier. You must not be observed. Ben Betiah is one of the leaders of the zealots and is being watched closely. Let no one see you bring him here. Go in peace, Joshua."

"May I wait with you, Rabban? There is something I have been reading that I do not understand."

A sad smile flickered on the old teacher's face. "Eliezer, you are like a well which never loses a drop of water. You never lose an opportunity to learn. Yes, we will wait and study together."

Illustrated by Lazlo Matulay

The sun was beginning to go down when Joshua returned with Rabban Johanan's nephew.

Ben Betiah was shocked at the change in his uncle's appearance. His hair and beard had grown snow-white. His
face was lined with worry. "It has been a long time since
I have seen you, Uncle."

"Two years, Ben Betiah. In this very room. Do you
remember what I told you then? That we had no need for
war with the Romans as long as they allowed us to study
and worship in peace. Study of the Torah, not war, is the
most important aim in life."

"Freedom! That, too, is important, Uncle. Not to have
to pay tribute to a foreign power and to live as we choose."

"At the cost of so many lives? Ben Betiah, listen to me.
Once again I have sent for you to ask that you help restore
peace in our land. As soon as the legions of Roman soldiers
enter our city no thing and no human being will be safe."

Ben Betiah bowed his head on his chest. When he looked
up there were tears in his eyes. "I wish it were possible for
me to bring peace, Uncle. But it is too late. The revolutionaries will not listen to me. They would only kill me.
Gladly would I give my life to stop the war, but the truth
is"—he spoke so softly now they had to lean forward to hear
him—"this war will be fought until one side or the other is
defeated."

"Then it is already too late to save Jerusalem. Go now
quickly before you are discovered here. And peace be with
you, Ben Betiah."

The room was quiet and they were alone again before
Rabban Johanan spoke. "It is too late to save the Holy
City. But one thing must be saved . . . Our Torah."

"How can we do that, Rabban? In all of Jerusalem, there
is only one teacher who has a knowledge of Torah above

all, and that is you. But you are trapped in the city just as we are."

"Our bodies are trapped. Our minds are free. This is a problem to be solved with the mind."

"No matter how we reason, there is still no way, Rabban, for you to leave the city."

The rabbi held up a thin hand. "Eliezer and Joshua, there is a way. But it is filled with danger. Not only to me but to both of you, for this is something I cannot do alone. I need your help. Together we may, if we are successful, save the Torah. Come closer and listen carefully. I will tell you the only way we may be able to take the teachings of Judaism out of Jerusalem."

*   *   *

The room was almost dark as Rabban Johanan ben Zakkai finished telling him how they could escape from Jerusalem. "Many of our teachings still are not written, but oral. They have been handed down from teacher to teacher. My lifetime has been spent memorizing these teachings. If I am killed when Jerusalem is defeated, all this knowledge dies with me."

Eliezer's face was tense. "We must get you out of the city before it is too late. But how?"

The old teacher's voice was calm. "Be at ease, Eliezer and Joshua. If we lose our heads in this time of crisis, we may lose our lives. Let me tell you the only way I can try to leave. As you know, nothing leaves the city, not even those who have died. They are thrown over the outer wall."

Joshua interrupted, "But for a great teacher like you, an exception might be made. So we will pretend you have died."

"Exactly, Joshua. Then you will take my body down to the gates and ask the guards for permission to take me out of the city for burial. If we succeed, we will be free. If we fail, or are discovered, it means death to us all."

"Rabban Johanan," both disciples said, "we are not afraid. And we will do everything we can to help."

Day by day, they worked on the details of their plan. In his room, Ben Zakkai practiced so that no part of his body moved; until he knew he could lie as still as if he were really dead.

Word was sent out to the people that the aged teacher was desperately ill. Although crowds gathered outside his home, no one was allowed to enter or serve him but his two disciples. A few days later, Joshua and Eliezer sadly informed the waiting throngs that the great leader, Johanan ben Zakkai, was dead.

Now the time had come to carry out the most dangerous part of the plan. The disciples laid the supposedly dead rabbi on a wooden bier. They covered him from head to toe. The rabbi lay rigid and unmoving as Joshua and Eliezer picked up the bier and went out into the street and made their way past wailing groups of people.

No one stopped them as they moved through the narrow streets. At one turning, an old woman sitting in her doorway called out between sobs, "Beloved Rabbi, I mourn not only thee, but my son fallen in battle. If only we had listened to thee, Jerusalem would have peace and I would still have my son."

Slowly Joshua and Eliezer approached the gate nearest the cemetery. When they saw the guards awaiting them, they felt icy with tension.

The guards were stern-faced as the two disciples paused before them and rested their burden.

"Halt," the older guard called. "Where do you think you are going with that coffin? You know the order as well as we do. You may leave the body here. We will get rid of it over the high outer wall."

Eliezer whose temper was as quick as his wits, answered, "That you will not do. This is the body of our beloved teacher, Rabban Johanan ben Zakkai. We ask only that we be allowed to give him decent burial."

The younger guard spoke quietly. "So Rabban Johanan is gone. May his soul rest in peace. I heard him speak once in the court of the hewn stones. I still remember his words. 'Live to learn Torah and you will learn how to live.' Ben Simon, surely for this man we can make an exception."

"You are as mad as they are. If we allow them to leave, tomorrow we may be as dead as he is." The crowds surrounding them began to wail again.

Ben Simon, the older guard, did not know what to do.

If he allowed them to leave, he could be punished for breaking the law of the zealots. Yet if he did not allow the sage to have a decent burial, he might be punished too. What was he to do?

"Very well," he roared, "I will allow you to pass on one condition. First I must stab the body just once, to make sure the old man is really dead."

Joshua quieted Eliezer with a look. Careful now, his eyes warned, our beloved Ben Zakkai's life is at stake. "You know the Jewish laws pertaining to death," he soothed in a quiet voice. "No body must be rudely touched in any way. If you do harm to Ben Zakkai, you will be guilty of breaking a law given by one greater than the revolutionaries."

Ben Simon put down his sword. The disciple was right. He could not stab or even push the body a little as he would like to do. Suddenly he remembered that the old man's nephew was Ben Betiah, one of the leaders of the rebels. He knew that Ben Betiah might personally avenge any disrespect shown to his beloved uncle.

Ben Simon looked at Judah. There was no help to be found from that young donkey. He certainly wasn't going to take the responsibility of such a matter on his head. "Very well," he said gruffly, "take him out and bury him. No one will ever say that I did not honor Johanan ben Zakkai. Be quick about it."

He was glad to be rid of such a problem, to see the crowds melt as the bier was carried through the gates and out of the city of Jerusalem.

They had risked their lives and won. More important than their lives, their teacher and the teachings of Judaism had been saved.

But their problems were not yet over. As they rested in

a cave outside Jerusalem, they discussed the last ordeal that faced them: how to obtain a city where they and other refugees could be safe in the future.

"There is no choice," said Rabbi Yohanan. "I must go to General Vespasian. His tent is pitched near here. He is the only one with authority to help us."

"Vespasian must remember how you urged peace," added Eliezer.

"That is so, Eliezer. However, I wanted peace because I thought it best for my people."

The aged teacher sighed. Their escape from the Holy City meant nothing, if they had no safe place to live and study. He did not want to see the man who was bringing so much grief and destruction to his people. Yet it had to be done.

Joshua interrupted his thoughts. "What city will you ask for, Rabban?"

What city! It must be one easily reached by the refugees. There must be scholars available to begin writing down the Holy Laws of Judaism to preserve them forever. A city where all could find shelter and employment. Where? Where?

"We will think about this problem while seeking Vespasian. Time is precious. Let us be on our way."

Vespasian was known to be a cruel, calculating man. Johanan ben Zakkai would have to be cautious in his dealings with him. The future of Judaism depended on whether Vespasian granted his request for a city. Would he? They walked down the road unafraid. For they had their faith and it gave them courage.

* * *

Over and over again Johanan ben Zakkai and his two disciples asked themselves this question: What city could prove to be a haven for the children of Judea? One after another, they discarded possible locations. One was too far away. Another offered no means of employment. So it went.

"We must come to a decision, since you are to see General Vespasian this afternoon, Rabban Johanan. Is there not one city in Palestine that meets our needs?" Joshua asked.

The rabbi, lost in thought, did not answer for a moment, then he said, "On the Mediterranean, there is a seaport city, known for its warm climate. We would not have to build an academy there, but could meet in the open."

"Rabban, surely we need more than a seaport and climate."

"That is so, Eliezer. Listen. This city is in the richest part of Palestine. Nearby are other cities where shelter and employment can be found. Also, many scholars have emigrated there, so we will have help in our holy work."

Joshua could not wait to hear more. "Rabban Johanan, you mean the city of Yavneh?"

"Yes. I go now to meet with Vespasian and I plan to ask for Yavneh as a refuge, a sanctuary. Whether he will grant our request or not remains to be seen."

The Roman soldiers looked with awe as the tall, gray-bearded teacher from Jerusalem was given the signal to enter Vespasian's tent. He must be important, or the General would not give him his valuable time.

Vespasian's face was unsmiling as he greeted Ben Zakkai. Life to the Roman general was a game of chance and he calculated each move greedily. "Welcome, Johanan ben Zakkai. You are a friend to Rome. I remember how you stood for peace."

"I was thinking then, General, as I now do of the welfare

of my people. Is there no hope for them?"

Vespasian's voice was cold. "Let us not bandy words. You are known for your wisdom, Rabbi. If you thought Jerusalem could be saved, you would not have left the city. Let me be brief. Once you tried to prevent the war. We are indebted to you for that. Now, tell me, why are you here?"

"I will also be brief, sir. For myself, I ask nothing. But I am here on behalf of my people. To ask for a city as a sanctuary."

Vespasian thought this remark over carefully. Was it worth it to Rome to give a city to Ben Zakkai? Yes, it was. He knew the rabbi would help later to bind up the wounds of the war-torn country. Now he said lightly, "What city were you thinking of?"

"Yavneh. We must be assured of its safety and that we will be allowed to live there in peace."

"For this you risked your life and those of your disciples? For the little city of Yavneh?" In his place, the General thought, I would have asked for riches and a palace.

"It may be a little thing to you, sir," Ben Zakkai said softly, "but to us it is a chance to renew our lives."

"So be it. The city is yours and your people will be able to live there in safety. You have my word." He looked at Ben Zakkai as he left with a feeling of deep respect.

At Yavneh the days passed swiftly. There was much to do. Ben Zakkai founded a school of Jewish learning—a yeshiva—which met in a shady vineyard. He organized the teachers into the Bet Din, which served as a court in place of the Sanhedrin.

So two years passed, with the news from Jerusalem becoming grimmer with the passage of time. The city was still besieged by the Romans. Then after a period of silence, a flow of wounded, starved refugees began flowing into Yavneh. The news they brought was tragic and terrible.

On the ninth day of Ab, in the year 70 C.E., Jerusalem had fallen. The ballista, great slingshots, had thrown torrents of stones into the city. Battering rams had broken through the walls. Torches had been put to the gates which burned and the city was then open to the enemy.

The Romans had been merciless. The young people of Judea had been taken as captives along with the sacred vessels from the Temple. All had been taken to Rome. Some of the young men were sent to fight wild animals in the Roman Colosseum. Coins had been struck to celebrate the victory, showing Judea as a desolate woman, surrounded by the inscription *Judea Capta* (captive Judea).

Finally, the brave leader of the zealots, Simon bar Giora, had been hurled from a rock, as a sacrifice to the Roman gods.

Rabban Johanan ben Zakkai, who had been listening to this tragic report told by a refugee, asked, "Tell me what happened to the Temple. Does it still stand unharmed?"

The refugee hesitated. "How can I tell you this, Rabban Johanan? An accident it was, true. But . . . our Temple has been destroyed."

The rabbi's face was pale. "What do you mean, destroyed?"

"Nothing remains of our beautiful Temple. A torch fell into one of the rooms. Though we fought the flames with our very lives, we could not put out the fire. The Temple burned to the ground. The Roman soldiers rolled the remaining stones into the Valley of Kidron."

Ben Zakkai spoke as if in pain. "Did you say nothing remains? You are wrong, my son. The temple is destroyed. The Holy City is rubble. Many of our people are in captivity. But our faith is strong and free in our hearts. And always will be." Overcome with grief, he went alone into his room.

For a whole day, Ben Zakkai did not appear. When he did, he called all his students to him.

"There are some things I must say. Not to mourn what has happened would be against nature. But to mourn too long would be unwise, too. The past and its glory is gone; but we must live in the present and look forward with hope to the future."

The students surrounding him were solemn. They nodded their heads in agreement as he continued. "The Temple is gone. Let us adapt ourselves to a new way of life. Prayer and charity will take the place of sacrifice. The synagogue will stand in place of the Temple. Here in Yavneh, we must continue to study and to teach those who wish to learn."

So it was. In the large vineyard at Yavneh, Johanan ben Zakkai and his disciples continued to train teachers for years to come. These teachers traveled all over the world to teach the Torah to the Jewish people wherever they were living in exile.

*   *   *

The class was silent as Rabbi Stein ended the lesson. They understood more than ever now what a privilege it was to study the spiritual and ethical lessons of the Torah. And they would always remember the man who risked his life so that the teachings of Judaism could live . . . Johanan ben Zakkai.

Eleazar the Maccabee

BY ROBERT GARVEY

CHEERING came up from the Temple Court, and the Syrians up in the Fortress tower at Acra jeered again at Eleazar.

"Hear, Eleazar—?" the Syrian captain was calling down to him—"how they hail Judah, the great Maccabee?"

"For fighting battles, Eleazar," another Syrian taunted him—"not for watching a fortress!"

Burning with shame, Eleazar left off checking the water bottles and arrows of his men standing guard around the fortress. Once and for all he would go to Judah and demand that he be allowed to lead fighting troops.

He did not see Judah at the Temple, though—only the working volunteers, dirty with sweat and dust. Some were digging out the stone altar on which the flesh of swine had been sacrificed. Some were on their knees scrubbing the tile floor with lye. Others were carrying out broken plaster of the Greek gods. As an extra-big piece of idol was dragged out of the court and dumped to the ground below, there was cheering.

"And what brings you here?"

The deep, warm voice was Judah's. Eleazar looked around: his brother was on his knees, a scrubbing brush in his hand.

"They mock me—and jeer at me."

Judah nodded. "They are angry, Eleazar. And they will be angrier when we rededicate our Temple. That is why you must build a wall, Eleazar—between the fortress and the Temple. Otherwise they will mock and jeer with arrows." Eleazar looked fiercely at Judah.

"I—I want to be a fighter."

"You are keeping the enemy garrison bottled up."

"That is not driving them out of the land."

Judah stood up and put his hand gently on his brother's tense shoulder. "You are worth many fighting generals, Eleazar. Where would brother Simon be, and Johanan and Jonathan and myself—without the food and supplies you bring us! We depend on you, Eleazar. You always do what has to be done."

And then, as if in answer to the question that was torturing Eleazar, Judah called out in his deep voice:

"Brothers! Countrymen! Who is fighting the war against the invaders?"

The hammers and brushes and spades and crowbars clattered to silence and the men answered back:

"We—the people."

"And who is your leader?"

"God—He is our leader."

"And you follow—?"

"The Maccabees."

"And which Maccabee is most important?"

There was some hesitation, then someone called out: "All of them!" "Yes, yes," the others took up the word: "All—all are important!"

Eleazar bowed his head.

"I shall build the wall," he said, softly.

And with the help of volunteers at the Temple and his own men, Eleazar did build a protecting wall around the Temple.

Now when the Temple was again clean, Jews came from the far corners of Judea, and there was rejoicing in the Temple Court while the Syrian garrison in Acra shrieked insults at the blank wall. And word of this heroic thing— that the Jews rededicated their Temple at Jerusalem while the nearby fortress was held by Syrian soldiers—spread throughout the world, and the Syrian king, Antiochus, was made a laughingstock. And the Jews took heart in their fight for freedom, so that army after army sent by Antiochus was slashed to pieces by the farm boys, shepherds, and other volunteers with the Maccabees.

And then one day Judah sent a messenger to Eleazar telling him that he was rushing to Bet Sura to battle Antiochus' newest army, and that Eleazar must guard the fortress with special vigilance, since the garrison might try to break out.

Word of the new army must have reached the garrison, for the Syrians broke into jeering again.

"Prepare to meet your death," they shouted to Eleazar and his men. "The conqueror Lysias is coming with an army of a hundred thousand!" And they shrieked that Lysias had the deadliest archers that gold could buy, the latest Roman engines of war, and more than a hundred battle-seasoned elephants. No arrows could pierce their thick hides. No human army could stop them. Let all the

Jews know that the end had come for Judea. "Enjoy your last hour on earth," they cried out. "Shall we send you down some wine? Better still—come up here and watch your Temple being leveled to the ground."

And one Syrian waved his sword drunkenly, crying out:

"Yahoo! The great Judah thinks the army is coming through Bet Sura, eh? Oh, no! We see fire signals. Lysias is coming through Bet Zechariah!"

Eleazar hurried to the spy tower of the Temple. The drunken Syrian had spoken the truth! While Judah and his men were on the way to Bet Sura, an endless line of troops that could only be Lysias' had swung away from there and was headed for Bet Zechariah.

It was too late to send word to Judah. And yet if Lysias were not stopped, he would march straight to the Temple and destroy it. What was to be done? What had to be done?

Eleazar posted five hundred of his guards in full view of the garrison. Then he led his five hundred other men behind the fortress tower, and under cover of the shade trees, he hurried on with them towards Bet Zechariah.

Illustrated by Lili Cassel Wronker

Soon sounds of the enemy army reached them, and some of his men began to lag, holding back out of fear.

Eleazar whispered, "Are you afraid, Jacob? And you, Naphtali? I am too, I am too." He paused, dampening his dry lips. "But the enemy—he must be afraid of *us*. Yes! That is why he has sent a hundred thousand men against us! And ferocious beasts! Hear them? Hear them?" . . . When he spoke again his eyes were bright and his words were bold. "Comrades!" he said. "Think! Today we can make a name for ourselves. If anyone here—in this hour of Judea's greatest danger—is satisfied with the name of Guard and Gatherer of Supplies, let him go home now. I know what I have to do!"

"We're with you, Eleaz—" the men began to shout, but this was cut short by the trembling of the ground as a dozen elephants came into sight.

Half of the men stared. The other half turned to run. Eyes flashing, Eleazar raised his sword for an attack—and his men came to their senses.

His archers strung their bows and let fly. Caught by surprise, several of the Syrian officers toppled off the forts on the elephants' backs. The animals wounded by the arrows screamed with rage and rushed at Eleazar's men with their metal-tipped tusks.

Eleazar's archers leaped back and drew their bows again; and the maddened, trumpeting beasts now thundered ahead, uprooting trees and trampling on everything in their path.

Eleazar did not know that the bellowing of the animals and the shouts and screams of the men had told Judah where the fighting was and that he would quickly come with the reinforcements. But the rest of the battle is known to history—how Eleazar noticed an elephant more elaborately armed than the rest, and thinking it carried Lysias himself, made his way under it and plunged his spear into its belly, bringing the giant beast down upon him and crushing all those riding upon it.

*   *   *

Through their magnificent bravery the Jews won peace and the right to worship in their Temple without bowing before the king's statue or eating the flesh of swine. And Eleazar, by doing what had to be done, had made a name for himself and his men forever.

A Menorah in Tel Aviv

BY YA'AKOV

"HEY, DAVID! What are you dreaming about?"

David blinked and saw his two friends sitting almost in front of him on the curb. Tel Aviv has some very busy streets, and he hadn't noticed his friends coming.

Joseph was still waiting for an answer. At last, David said, "About a menorah for Hanukkah."

What he did not tell the boys was that he was trying to think of a way to ask his father about a menorah. They had thrown out their old metal one when mother had been housecleaning before the summer. It had been bent and rusty, and the wax drippings from last year's colored candles were still stuck on it. He remembered father saying, "By next Hanukkah I'll surely have a job and then we will buy a beautiful new menorah."

But only last night, when David was about to remind his father, the dog-eared record book with the family budget was open on the table. David saw his father chewing the end of his pencil. He knew what that meant. There wasn't much work in the building trade these days. David swallowed his words and left the house.

Reuben broke in on his thoughts. "We were just talking about Hanukkah lamps, too," he said.

"Not just about any old menorah," Joseph corrected him. "Think of it, David, they are going to build a giant steel tower right here in the center of Tel Aviv. Maybe like the Eiffel Tower in Paris! And on top will be a mighty Hanukkah lamp. Each light will be a million candlepower! The papers said so today. All of Tel Aviv will be lit!"

David's face lit with sudden joy. "Really?" he cried. "If . . . if that's so. we won't have to light a menorah in our homes!"

Joseph roared, "You believe everything, don't you! Didn't you realize that I was just joking?"

"And even if they would build a giant-size Hanukkah lamp I would still want to light candles of my own," said Reuben. "You ought to see how beautiful our menorah is —it's all hammered silver, decorated with lions and birds, and the candle-holders are small and graceful."

"Our Hanukkah lamp uses oil," said Joseph. "You pour

a little oil into each holder and light it. And then I ask my father to place the lamp on the window sill that faces the street, and I go down to the street and look up at our window."

David closed his eyes and said, "I think it would be wonderful to build a giant menorah. When I grow up and become an engineer I will build a huge tower in the center of Tel Aviv. I'll put a great menorah on top of it and each candle will shine with the power of a million candles and nobody will have to light his own menorah at home. On Hanukkah everyone will be amazed, because the night will be as bright as day."

"Say, I've got an idea," Reuben broke in. "Suppose we all go out on the first day of Hanukkah and look at the windows of all the homes to see who has the most beautiful menorah."

"Swell!" cried Joseph.

"Nothing could be more beautiful than a real giant menorah," David said, with a break in his voice.

Finally, he gave in. He could not tell his friends his troubles. Maybe there wouldn't even be a Hanukkah lamp at all in his house this year. And even if there would be one—it surely would not be made of hammered silver or burn pure olive oil.

Until the very day before Hanukkah, David had no chance to speak to his father about a menorah. His father had still not found any work. David nibbled his bread and cheese and wondered how to start the conversation. At last, after a small pile of green olive pits had accumulated on his father's plate, he suddenly said, "Dad, what do you think? Would it be possible to build a giant menorah at the top of a tower in the center of Tel Aviv, with a million candlepower for each light?"

"What for?" his father asked. "Where did you get such an idea?"

"If there would only be a menorah like that, everyone would be able to go outside and enjoy it. We wouldn't need our own menorah. Then those who could not afford a beau-

Illustrated by Lili Cassel Wronker

tiful menorah of hammered silver would not be"—he finished bravely—"ashamed of their tin menorah."

The father studied his son's face for quite a while. Then
he lowered his glance and poked with his fork at the pile
of pits in his plate.

"A giant menorah," he said slowly. "No, David, there is
no need for it. I understand your thoughts, my son. But
the beauty of a menorah is in its small lights. They fill the
whole house with a warm glow and they remind every single
family of the wonderful Hanukkah story. Best of all is lighting them with your own hands so that you can see their
little flames flicker."

"Father, tell me," David interrupted, "what kind of
menorah will you buy?"

"Wait and see," answered his father with a steady voice.

David was on edge all day. He kept glancing at the clock
on the dresser. When it began to grow dark and the Hanukkah lights started to flicker in the neighboring homes,
David's father arose and said: "Bring a stout plant of wood,
David, and nine potatoes from the pantry." Then he reached into his pocket and opened a penknife.

David soon returned with the board and potatoes.

"Take the knife," said his father, "and split each potato
in half. In each half carve a hole big enough to set a candle
into. We'll place the halves on the board and we will have
a menorah."

David didn't know whether to laugh or cry. He took the
knife and started to cut and carve. As he worked with the
first potato, it seemed silly to him. With the second one,
he tried to cut evenly and smoothly and with the third he
enjoyed the idea. A potato menorah! Who ever heard of
such a remarkable menorah!

The shammash candle stood firm in its holder.

The first candle stood upright too. And when his father started to sing *Ma-oz Tzur,* the two flames danced and so did their images in the windowpanes.

A few minutes later, David ran towards his frends in the street. Before they could say a word, he cried out: "What a menorah we've got! You never saw anything like it! It's made of potatoes and it's homemade and . . ."

"Potatoes?" said Reuben. "I never heard of a potato menorah."

"Potatoes?" snickered Joseph. "What will you do with your menorah after Hanukkah? Eat it?" He burst into laughter.

David's spirits refused to be dampened.

"Look at the lights," he pointed to his window. In the

back of the menorah he saw the blurry image of his father standing behind the lights.

"My father created that menorah," said David proudly. "It shines with a bright and beautiful light. To me, it's the most beautiful menorah in the whole world."

His voice trembled and his wide eyes glistened. Joseph and Reuben looked at him as though they were seeing him for the first time. Then they gazed long and hard at the potato menorah and at the shadow of David's father.

"You know," whispered Reuben, "when you think of it, it is a beautiful menorah."

And Joseph nodded his head in agreement.

The Stones

BY FRIEDA CLARK HYMAN

MOST OF ALL Shalom remembered Azariah's father. He had led his family into the *Ma'abarah*—the temporary camp for immigrants—carrying one package so proudly it might have been the Sacred Ark itself. Behind him Azariah's tiny mother had struggled with bundles so huge they had covered most of her body and face.

Now, Shalom was not shocked by the sight of women working. He himself was a Yemenite, and he knew how hard his own mother labored. Yet that had been too much. He could have kicked the man.

A few days later, Mr. Dan brought Azariah to his class. "Boys," Mr. Dan said, "this is Azariah. He comes from Amadiyah."

"Where is Amadiyah?" Shalom called out.

Mr. Dan smiled. "Tell them, Azariah," he said.

But the new boy would not utter a syllable.

"Never mind," Mr. Dan patted the boy's shoulder. "You will learn Hebrew soon." And pointing to Shalom, he said, "Let Azariah share your bench, Shalom. You're almost the same age."

It was not easy making friends with this silent boy. But Shalom understood. He could still remember how strange this old-new land had seemed to him. Besides he was a curious lad. And he still hadn't learned where Amadiyah was.

Gradually Azariah learned Hebrew. And with each new word, he became less distant. Until one morning, he actually spoke first.

"Would you like to go for a ride with us tomorrow?" he asked.

"A ride? In what?"

"In the truck, of course."

"But how can you get the truck?"

"Mr. Dan arranged it. We are going to the Negev. There's a farm for us there."

"But you're not a farmer yet?"

Azariah smiled. "Of course I'm a farmer," he said. "All my people are."

"But who exactly are your people?" Shalom asked. "And where," he cried, "where is Amadiyah?"

"In Kurdistan. We are Kurdish Jews of Iraq, of the tribe of Naphtali."

"Naphtali!" Shalom was suddenly angry at such showing off. "How can you know what tribe you come from? Naphtali was one of the lost ten tribes. Everyone knows they disappeared."

"That's what most believe. But it isn't true. We know."

"Know something that happened . . ." Shalom struggled

to figure out the date of that first captivity.

"Over twenty-five hundred years ago," Azariah helped him.

"Twenty-five hundred years ago! And you still want me to believe you belong to Naphtali?"

"It's the truth, Shalom. You see my ancestors never left the places to which we were taken. In our hills the tribes of Dan, Asher, Zebulon and Naphtali settled."

"What hills?"

"The hills of Nisbur. Where Shalmaneser, King of Assyria, took us."

"I still can't believe it."

"But Shalom, we still speak the same language."

"You don't. You're just learning Hebrew."

"That's true. Because we spoke Aramaic. Like in the Talmud. It was the language of Kurdistan."

Shalom was silent. To speak the language of the Talmud filled him with awe. "And all of you remained farmers?" he finally asked. "As you had been in ancient Israel?"

"And my father can't wait to begin farming again."

Suddenly Shalom remembered: Azariah's father carrying only one package, while his tiny wife had struggled with a huge load. "Ha!" he said sharply. "Your father! He work! He farm! Don't make me laugh!"

The next thing he knew he was looking up at Azariah. His jaw ached and Azariah was arched over him, fists ready.

"Get up," Azariah prodded him with his foot. "Get up so I can knock you down again."

Like a cat, Shalom sprang at Azariah. Hips twisting, fists flying, the boys circled each other. How long they might have gone on, they would never know.

Two arms held each boy upright and apart. "Well, now," Mr. Dan studied them, "and I thought you were friends."

"He insulted me," Azariah flared.

"And he's a liar," Shalom cried.

"Insulted. Liar." Mr. Dan shook his head. "That's strong language." He released them. "Here, come out of this hot sun into my office. Let's talk it over."

When they were on opposite sides of his desk, Mr. Dan began. "You know, boys," he said, "you've both returned

Illustrated by Hovav Kruvi

to Israel after hundreds of years. You, two thousand years, and you, Azariah, after twenty-five hundred. You, Shalom, from the south, and you, Azariah, from the north. And here you are after all that time and space, fighting. Does that make sense?"

"He had no right to insult my father," Azariah protested.

"No one has. That is," he looked at Shalom, "if he really did."

"All I said," Shalom muttered, "was his father wouldn't work."

"See!" Azariah went out of his chair.

"Hold on!" Mr. Dan shoved Azariah back. "And you, Shalom," he added sternly, "how do you know what Azariah's father would or wouldn't do?"

"I saw him," Shalom said. "I saw him when he came into the *Ma'abarah*. He carried one package, while his wife . . . well you couldn't even see her behind her load."

"Pillows!" Azariah cried. "Goose feathers."

"Oh." Shalom felt his ears tingle with shame. "It looked . . . so enormous . . ."

"And do you know what Azariah's father bore?" Mr. Dan asked quietly.

"No, sir." Shalom's eyes sought the floor.

"Would you like to know?"

"Yes, sir."

"Will you tell him, Azariah?"

"NO!"

"I . . . I'm sorry, Azariah," Shalom whispered.

Mr. Dan waited. Then he asked again. "Will you tell Shalom now, Azariah? Will you tell him what your father carried?"

Shalom hardly dared to breathe. Would Azariah ever speak to him? Could they be friends again?

"My father," Azariah said, "carried stones."

"Stones!" Shalom's eyes widened with astonishment. "Did you say *stones?*"

"I said stones."

"But, what good are stones?"

Azariah stared into distances. "They are holy stones. The stones of our synagogue of Amadiyah, Bet Yehezkel. We took it apart, before we left, stone by stone."

"But why," Shalom asked, "why should you do that?"

"Rather than let unclean hands touch it. My ancestors

built it according to the directions in the Book of Ezekiel."

"But weren't those the instructions on how to build the Temple?"

"That's how we built our synagogue. Just like the Temple."

"Did you draw the plans before you destroyed it, Azariah?"

"No," Azariah said. "We didn't."

Shalom could have wept. "But why? We could have had a model for our future Temple!"

"Have you forgotten, Shalom?" Mr. Dan smiled. "We still have the Book of Ezekiel in the Bible."

Shalom relaxed. A wonderful sense of peace flooded his being. The Ten Tribes and their ancient language were not lost after all. They had remained farmers all these years, even building a miniature Temple.

And now one day, perhaps, the stones of that ancient synagogue could be set into a new, and enduring Temple in Israel.

"Azariah," he asked happily, "will you take me with you tomorrow? I want to see that farm too."

"Yes, Shalom."

"And the stones, Azariah. Will you let me see them too?"

"Yes, Shalom."

And neither Shalom nor Azariah noticed Mr. Dan had left his office.

What Happened to Ovadya

BY A. A. DAVIDSON

EVERY MORNING at ten o'clock the whistle blew on the train going up to Jerusalem. Ovadya and I put down our hoes, with which we had been weeding rows of vegetables. We sat underneath the big eucalyptus tree and had a drink of cold tea. Ovadya didn't usually talk very much, but one morning, when we were sitting under the tree, he suddenly said:

"Now I am going to tell you a story about something that happened to me when I was a boy in Yemen. Pay attention now."

Ovadya wears a sort of turban around his head. He took it off and wiped his dark face with it. Then he wound it around his head again. That's one of the useful things about a turban. You couldn't do that with a hat. I saw that

Ovadya's hair was as gray as his beard and his *peot*—one on each side of his head, in front of his ears. He had very bright dark eyes, and he looked at me and said:

"First of all, you must understand that in Yemen there were only Jews and Arabs, and the Arabs were all Mohammedans. We were both very religious people, but the Mohammedans only wanted that the Jews should become Mohammedans too. They had a trick for that, but you must pay attention carefully if you want to hear what it was.

"So this is what happened once when I was a boy, in Yemen. My father—peace be upon him—was very sick. I was just a little boy and did not know how very sick he was. And he wanted to smoke his big water pipe, but when I looked in the jar there was no toombac for the pipe. So my father sent me to the market place to buy some toombac . . . What? You don't know what toombac is? Why, that is what you smoke in pipes and cigarettes. Of course!

"I bought the toombac and started to go back home. In the street I met a man who lived in the house next to ours, and he took me by the hand.

" 'Come with me quickly, Ovadya!' he said, speaking close to my ear in a low voice. And he walked so fast that I could hardly keep up with him. We went into a different street, and suddenly a door opened, and he pushed me inside and closed the door. I could hear him shouting outside.

" 'Come back, Ovadya!' he shouted. 'Don't run away! Wicked boy, come back with the money!' and I could hear the sound of his feet, running—as if he was pretending to be running after me—but I was inside the house, and someone was holding me. He let me loose, and I turned around and saw that he was a black man, such as the Arabs used to bring back from Africa to be slaves for them. The black man smiled at me, a sad smile, and I knew he had a good heart˙towards me.

" 'Poor Ovadya!' he said. 'Now you are an orphan, for your father is dead, too. He has just died, and that is why you must hide.'

"Pay attention now, and I will explain what he meant. My mother—peace be upon her—had died when I was a baby, and I was raised by my father's second wife. Now, this is the trick I told you the Arabs in Yemen had, to make Jews become Mohammedans: the Arabs there had a law, that if a Jewish child became an orphan before he was twelve years old, they then took him away to be raised as a Mohammedan. Now I understood that my father must have known that he was dying, and sent me away on purpose. I understood that my neighbors had arranged to hide me with the black man until the Jews could smuggle me away to another city.

"I was afraid, and I cried. When I was finished crying, I asked him, 'Why are you helping to hide me? If you are caught the Arabs will punish you. Why do you do it for me, a Jewish boy you never saw before?'

"He said, 'Because when I was no older than you, I was taken away from my own country, from Africa, and brought here to be a slave. And I, too, never saw my father again.'

"Well, the Arabs in the city looked everywhere for me, but they never thought of looking in a non-Jew's house, so they never found me.

"Then one day the black man came in with a big basket. He asked me if I could fit inside it, and I crawled into the basket and lay down in it. He covered me with dried figs. Then he filled another basket with figs, and he fastened the two baskets on the back of a camel, and we went out of the city. For four days I stayed in the basket. It was not safe for me to come out, even at night.

"Then we came to another city and the black man sold the two baskets of figs to a Jew. He bent down, as if to fix his sandal, and he said, very softly, 'Farewell, Ovadya,' and I whispered, 'Farewell.' When the Jew had brought the figs into his own courtyard, and barred the doors, he took off the figs and he lifted me out. But I could not walk, my legs were so stiff from being in the basket those four days. This man's name was Zacharya, and there was a girl with him.

" 'Miryam,' he said to the girl, 'get me the oil.' And she did and her father rubbed my legs with the oil, and my arms, until the blood began to move in them again. And so, after a while, I was able to walk again. And I went to work with Zacharya. After three more years, when I was fourteen, and a grownup man, I married Miryam.

"And now the only thing to add is to tell how we left Yemen and came here. After many years, the Arabs began to say that there was a war in Falastina against the Jews; and we Jews were afraid. And then we heard that the Jews had driven off the Arabs in Falastina, and the Arabs in

Yemen looked at us with new eyes, and we said, 'This is the hand of the Almighty.' The King of Yemen died then, and his son was the new king, and he heard of all these thing, and he said to us, 'I do not prevent you from leaving . . .' So we knew that the Lord was gathering us. We sold our property and put on our best clothes and took our Sifrei Torah in our arms and crossed the desert and the mountains until we came to the Land of Aden. There the King of England rules, not the King of Yemen.

"And we saw the great airplanes come down from the heavens to carry us to the land of Israel. We remembered the verse in the Torah which says 'You have seen how I carried you on eagle's wings, and brought you unto Myself,' and we said 'We have seen, Lord, we have seen!'—for one morning we had our breakfast in Aden, we went into the airplane with its eagle's wings—zzzzuuuummm! and we had our dinner in Israel!

"So that is the story of what happened to me in Yemen. I hope that you have paid attention to me, and that you will remember it. Formerly, I was an old man, but now I am in my own country I have been born again. Let us pick up our hoes and go back to work, for the work is not finished, and the people must not go hungry just because we have been talking."

We Saw the New Moon

"JOSEPH, will they believe us that we saw the new crescent moon, this time?"

"Yes, Dan. They will recognize us as having been among the witnesses last month at the Bet Yaazek courtyard, and they will accept us as honest people."

"But why did they not accept our testimony last time?"

"We were not known to them then. The rabbis must be certain that the evidence is true. There are too many false witnesses and troublemakers who want to confuse our people so that we will not know just when the holidays will fall."

The two boys sat with their backs against a tree high on the Mount of Olives. Below and away spread the city of Jerusalem.

"And what will happen, Joseph, if we don't see the new moon?"

"Then the rabbis will automatically declare tomorrow as Rosh Hodesh, the beginning of the month."

"How are they so sure of that?"

"Tonight is the thirtieth night since the last new moon was seen. On this evening the rabbis of the Sanhedrin gather to await the news of the new moon. If the new moon appears tonight, this day, the thirtieth of the month, will be declared the New Month; the last month will then have contained only twenty-nine days. If the moon is not seen, the day after will be the New Month, for no month may possibly be longer than thirty days."

The boys were silent for awhile. Then, "See, Joseph, there it is!" Dan pointed to a bright baby crescent that seemed to peep out of the blue edge of the mountain.

Joseph and Dan watched the moon float up. They studied the size, location, and shape of the young crescent.

"And now, Joseph, let us run to the Court of the Rabbis, to tell them that we saw the new moon."

The boys raced to Bet Yaazek to the Court of the Sanhedrin in Jerusalem. The doors were wide open. Inside the rabbis were seated in a semi-circle. To their great joy, they saw that they were the first to arrive. Not far behind they saw other witnesses running.

"Joseph, let's run faster. We've got to be the first this time."

They raced into the courtyard and rushed up to the rabbis, crying:

"Our lords and masters, we wish to report that we saw the birth of the new moon."

A tall man with a gray beard arose and said: "Let the older come near."

Illustrated by Lazlo Matulay

Joseph approached the semi-circle. Dan was led away out of earshot so that he could not hear his friend's report.

At last the rabbi said:

"Let the younger approach the court and give testimony."

Dan approached the Great Sanhedrin of seventy-one rabbis, the highest court of the land.

"Tell us, son," said an elder of the rabbis, "how did you see the moon? Before the sunset or after? To the north or to the south? How high was it? How broad was it?"

The rabbis peered intently at his face. They hung on his every word as he began his story. When he was finished the elder took out a group of tablets bearing pictures of different shapes of the moon.

"Tell us, Dan, did you see the moon like this, or like this, or perhaps like this?"

Dan pointed, "Like this."

"The Lord bless thee and guard thee, my son," said the elder.

Now the rabbis drew together in discussion. They all looked pleased and confident. Again the elder stepped forth, and raising his hand for silence he called in a loud voice: "We declare the month hallowed."

"It is hallowed," echoed all the rabbis and the people in the court.

"Let the messengers speed forth immediately to all our brethren in Israel, Syria, Babylonia and wherever they may live and proclaim that the new moon has been seen. The New Month has begun!"

Long is the Way to Jerusalem

IN THE OFFICE of the Eilat police station in Israel stood an annoyed, black-eyed boy. From his Yemenite Arabic, the police officers could only make out that he had come thirteen hundred miles on foot, all alone. Finally a Yemenite fisherman was called in and he began to interpret:

"They used to call me Dawood, but my real name is David Ben-Ezra Damari," said the boy. "*Damari* because I come from the City of Damar; and *Ben-Ezra* because Shafica said that my father's name was Ezra." When the pieces were put together, his history went somewhat like this:

It was a cool, quiet night; even the jackals did not feel like howling. Suddenly a harsh grip had shaken David out of his sleep and he faced Shafika. He followed her into the courtyard and they sat down on the huge grindstone.

On Shafika's palm—glittering in the moonlight like the blade of a knife—lay a peculiar, six-pointed star on a leather band. She explained that this was the star of the Jews and was called a Magen David.

"I am not your mother, Dawood," she said. "You are a Jew. Your parents died in the Great Sickness which struck that region when you were still a baby." She fastened the Magen David round his neck. "Your real mother—her name was Rachel—left this for you. Her last wish was that on the thirteenth spring of your life you shall be in the land of the Jews; in the Holy City of Jerusalem."

"*Ya-Allah!* The Holy City? But how do I get there?"

"It's a long, long way to the north," Shafika said, pressing a few coins into his hand. "To be there in time you must go now. Go, and Allah be with you . . ."

72

A last embrace and—on went David, leaving behind the slumbering city of Damar.

At daybreak he reached a village in the mountains. The dreary song of women who were grinding corn echoed through the fresh morning. He approached several of them, asking for the way to Jerusalem. Their shrewd eyes glared at him from behind the black veils, but they only shrugged and continued singing.

In the last clay hut of the village, an old woman pointed with her bony hand: "There, son, go north and Allah be with you."

Exhausted and thirsty, David reached Tuah, a town at the foothills of the A-Sarat mountains, which he intended to cross. After he quenched his thirst from the water of the public rain-barrel, he bought dry lamb, pittah-bread and a huge skin bottle: the equipment for his journey.

In Tuah he learned of something he had never thought about before: borders. And what was the usual penalty for smuggling across a border? It was—"chopping off." Of what? A hand, an ear, a head—no one cared in particular.

The most disturbing fact of all, though, was that he had to smuggle across many borders in order to reach Jerusalem. And the first one had to be braved that very night!

But he was caught.

Nothing helped. Neither the Magen David to which he prayed nor the tears which he shed in an attempt to soften the guard's heart and grip. So he was being carried off to be chopped. Chopped! David summoned all his courage and strength, tore his hand from the guard's grip, and plunged into the nearby wheatfield.

The bullets swished by. A sudden slap and pull . . . and a warm liquid began to flow down his left thigh and ankle.

David did not remember how long he lay there on the

soft, warm earth. Only when his heart beat normally again, did he realize that the bullet had hit only his skin bottle; that not blood but water had wet his ankle. So after all, perhaps the Magen David had saved him.

In the morning David bought a new skin bottle from a passerby and continued his journey over the A-Sarat mountains.

The nights he spent in caves and kept a fire alight, to keep the mountain beasts away. During the day he climbed. The higher he went, the steeper the path became, the barer the mountains, and the lonelier the way. The huge eagles and ugly vultures in the clear sky frightened him. But he continued; it was his mother's last wish—he must fulfill it!

After almost a month of walking, he saw that the barren path began to wind downward. The mountains turned gentler, the slopes greener, inhabited. How happy David was to see human beings again. He had almost forgotten what they looked like.

Arriving in the city of Akhroum, in Saudi Arabia, he again inquired about the way to Jerusalem. "North," was the answer. The passersby gazed curiously at the boy who would not tell why he wanted to get to Jerusalem. Stubbornly David continued on the main road towards the kingdom of Hejaz.

But after nearly three months, David's strength began to fail him. His clothes were in rags, his shoes torn, his feet sore and bleeding. Yet he continued. But he reached only the gates of the city of Taif. There a kind passerby found him, lying in the dust and weeping.

Fed and wrapped in a comfortable blanket, David told the stranger his story.

His host was a Jew—the first Jew David had ever spoken to. He listened patiently and then said, "I have an idea."

It was the season of the annual pilgrimage to the Holy
City of Mecca. Why not go to Mecca, mix with the crowd
and join a group whose way home (northward through the
Arabian peninsula) would lead David into the kingdom of
Jordan—only one border-smuggle from Jerusalem!

Mecca was crowded with pilgrims from every country in
the Arab world. Soon David made friends with a Syrian
group. They let him sleep under their blankets, eat their
food, and drink the milk of their camels. After the completion of their religious services in Mecca, they set out on
their way back north.

A monotonous month of plodding through the towns and
villages parallel to the shores of the Red Sea passed as if in
a dream. Then the pilgrims crossed the border of the kingdom of Jordan, into the city of Qualat al-Maudawara. The
same night David slid from under the heavy blankets and
out of the encampment.

Three weeks later he was in the town of Aqaba.

Eilat was just at the opposite side of the Gulf of Aqaba.

Illustrated by William Sayles

At night its lights flickered and twinkled invitingly; they seemed so close, as if only within an arm's length. David waited until the last lights disappeared in Aqaba and in Eilat. Then he started off, towards the last and best-guarded border.

The sand and gravel crackled and whispered under his feet. The sweat of fear wet his forehead. His hand clutched the Magen David. " . . . Not now, at the last border . . ." he pleaded in a whisper, "please . . ."

Suddenly a harsh hand grasped David's shoulder. Another hand pressed on his mouth and the cold steel of a weapon tickled his spine. He had run straight into a cordon of rifle barrels. Then, quietly, he was put on a truck among dark, silent figures which smelled of grass and gunpowder.

"And that's how I got here," David finished his story. "But they wouldn't believe me!" He unbuttoned his shirt. On his bony chest hung a small, rusty Magen David: "I *am* a Jew . . . honestly I am . . ."

Hector

BY HERMONA SIMON

IN 1947 we lived in our little house in Z'fon-Talpiot, a suburb of Jerusalem. The "suburb" consisted of six tiny little houses, each surrounded by a nice and very tiny little garden with trees as old as the houses. We built them in 1936.

One day, our son David, age eighteen, brought home a beautiful tiny boxer puppy. The puppy came from a very well-known canine family with an aristocratic pedigree. This family used Greek names, so we turned to mythology for a name, and decided on Hector, hero of ancient Troy.

The tiny little puppy grew amazingly and soon became a strong and powerful boxer. It was November, 1947. The peoples of the world, through their representatives at the United Nations, decided to divide Palestine into two states: a Jewish and an Arab one. The Palestinian Arabs opposed this decision violently, and trusting in their superior numbers and in support by the seven neighboring Arab states, attacked the Jews. In Jerusalem hostilities started on the third of December. In Z'fon-Talpiot, our six little houses on top of a hill, surrounded by large Arab quarters and villages, were in a very dangerous situation. Our men had to keep constant watch by day and by night. After a week or so of such a life we all became very tired.

It was then that Hector decided that he, too, had to take his share in the defense of his home. He was then exactly seven months old, and had never been trained. But he

Illustrated by Gabe Josephson

sensed from where the danger came and when David went to sleep, completely exhausted, Hector went on keeping watch. Thanks to Hector, Z'fon-Talpiot was never taken by surprise and we were able to withstand every attack. Gradually Hector learned to recognize the different arms used. He knew that it was easier to take cover from rifle shots and that machine-gun fire should be carefully avoided. He learned that land mines could be smelled from afar and that they were the worst enemies of his master.

The fighting developed into real war. David became a sergeant in a reconnaissance company. He was sent to a very lonesome outpost facing the Egyptian lines. In view of the dangerous position he decided to leave Hector at home. But David was only one day in his new place, when he suddenly saw his Hector arriving at his dugout, very happy at having found him. Of course, he stayed.

One day our son went on reconnaissance, Hector at his side. After about one mile of careful walking the dog became restless and tried to stop his master from going further. He jumped and barked, and David was almost angry with him. Suddenly the dog left David and bolted off in the exact direction David meant to go. It all went very quickly. Hector was about half a mile away when an explosion occurred. David started after his dog and, when the smoke cleared, he saw the poor creature gravely wounded by a land mine on which he had stepped. Hector had smelled the mine, but he could not stop David. So the faithful dog, at the risk of his own life, exploded the mine before David reached the danger spot.

David took the bleeding dog back to his post. A veterinary surgeon served in the same unit, and Hector was nursed back to health. After two years of military service both David and Hector returned home safe and sound. But, like every able-bodied Israeli citizen, Hector is still kept on the reserve list of the Israel Defense Forces, and whenever David and his father are called up for duty. Hector, too, joins his special canine unit. As a war veteran, he enjoys certain privileges, which in his case means an extra ration of meat, and that is a lot in these days!

The Lost Scroll

BY ELEAZER FREED

THE GOLDMAN twins were gloriously happy.

Father had brought the good news. He had come home and said, looking rather pleased, "It's settled."

"Of course, it will have to be third class," Father went on. "Business in London isn't that good at present."

"That doesn't matter, dear," said Mrs. Goldman.

By now this was too much for the twins!

"Id's nod fair keebig all thad secred ad nod delling us!" exclaimed Joseph hotly. (He was suffering from a very bad cold.)

"Why, Joseph, I really am sorry," said Father. "I quite forgot that you know nothing about it. Well, now, can you try and guess?"

"I can guess," cried Michael, the other twin, excitedly, "It's Israel. We're going at last to Israel!!"

"Right," agreed Father, "you have guessed it. We are going there in the spring—at Pesah—the finest time of all to visit Israel. Aunt Malka is going to put us up on the farm near Gedera."

When Sara, their elder sister, returned home later, the twins were delirious. Israel! It really was wonderful.

Two sunburnt boys stood upon a small plateau high in the Judean hills and made encouraging noises to a girl, slightly older than themselves, who climbed towards them. Before them and about them lay the brilliant panorama of the Israeli countryside. In the foreground, cultivated farms, orange groves, and orchards, looking as if painted in vivid colors, melted away towards the deep blue of the Mediterranean Sea. Through the clear, sweet air came the bleating of sheep, some of which were grazing high up on the hillside.

"I'm so glad I came now," said Sara, "It was worth it just for this."

Since coming to Israel, the Goldman family had done lots of sightseeing. But when they had had enough of that, the twins had received permission to make some *tiyulim* (excursions) on their own, under strict instructions to be back each evening well before dark. On one of these expeditions, they had climbed up to this particular plateau, and had discovered the opening of a cave almost concealed by a huge rock. They had no kind of light at the time, so they could only guess at its nature, but it seemed quite large inside and certainly worth exploring.

So they had come back now, together with Sara, and furnished with all the equipment thought necessary for such a venture—flashlights, rope, twine, and of course food and drink.

"I'll go first," said Michael, "Sara next, and Joseph last."

It seemed a sensible plan and they arranged themselves accordingly. Perhaps it was not strictly necessary for them to have roped themselves together, but they did so and felt better when, a moment or so later, they stood in the emptiness and silence of the large cave entrance.

At an immense height above their heads the walls tapered

together into a rocky cleft. A dim light seeped through from above.

Joseph's flash soon discovered an opening about six feet from the ground and he climbed up the rocky wall towards it.

"It's a sort of passage," he cried down to the others. "Shall I go through?"

"No, wait! We must fix the twine first," answered Michael. "Besides, we agreed that I should go first."

"Oh, all right," said Joseph, and having fastened one end of the twine securely round a huge boulder on the dusty floor of the cave, they started off.

After several hundred yards the passage broadened suddenly, and they saw they had reached another cave. An intensely foul smell struck their nostrils.

"Phew!" said Michael.

The word was barely out of his mouth when a black

Illustrated by Ben Einhorn

shape flung itself upon him and struck the flashlight from his hand! It fell to the ground and went out at once.

"Bats!" said Michael. "Thank goodness, they are harmless. Keep still, I'll try to find my flash."

He fumbled for a few minutes.

"Here it is!" he called out after a moment. "It's broken, though."

"What shall we do?" said Joseph.

"Oh, let's go back! whimpered Sara. "I'm so frightened!"

So they retraced their steps, not using the extra flashlight because of the bats.

"I think we ought to go back after lunch," said Joseph, after they had climbed out.

"When we get to the cave, we'll switch off the flashlight and feel our way through."

"I suppose that's the only way. What do you say, Sara?"

"Not me! I shall stay here until you come out."

So they all ate heartily and then the twins, after promising to come out again after two hours, disappeared into the cave.

By the time five o'clock came, Sara felt sure something dreadful had happened.

So she wrote a few words on a piece of paper and left this under a small mound of stones which she piled in front of the cave.

Beneath Sara's feet at this very moment were the Goldman twins!

They had penetrated beyond the cave of bats as they had planned, feeling their way without light so as not to disturb the creatures, but as they went, releasing the twine across the uneven and rocky floor.

Now they were standing in a tunnel where the use of

their flashlight was again possible.

The tunnel led upwards.

"It's man-made," declared Michael, when he saw the chipped, even nature of the walls, and they continued their climb with mounting excitement. But it was Joseph who made the first great discovery—a smooth, flat surface like a tablet was inset in the wall above his head!

At his cry Michael stopped and together they examined it. It was oblong in shape, made of some kind of cement, and upon it were six words clearly inscribed.

"It's not Hebrew," said Michael, "although this letter looks a bit like an *aleph* and so does this one."

"Perhaps it's a sort of warning," said Joseph.

Michael took out his notebook and carefully copied the inscription. He put the paper into his diary and they went on.

After a few more yards, the passage turned abruptly to the left and flattened out, and there in front of them, completely blocking it, was a carved, wooden door! Under the pressure of both their bodies, the door gave way suddenly, and they fell forward into a mass of ashes and rubble.

They turned their flash on the floor of the cell and saw thousands of parchment scrolls of all sizes. These must have been lying there for a very long period because for the most part they had disintegrated into powdered fragments.

"Look!" cried Michael, examining a few of the fragments on the palm of his hand. "Some of them have got the same kind of writing as that tablet."

"I believe I have seen these letters before," he added a moment later. "This is ancient Hebrew. Don't you remember—they've got some on Israeli stamps."

Then Michael had a stroke of luck! He actually had with him stuck into the pocket of his diary two Israeli stamps, and on one of these was the picture of an old Hebrew coin.

He was right! Unmistakably the letters on all these were the same.

"And now I know where we are," he went on. "This place is a Genizah."

"A—what?" said Joseph. Even the word had a scary sound in that scary place!

*   *   *

"What's a Genizah?" asked Joseph.

"Don't you remember?" Michael said. "A Genizah is a place where they store old manuscripts. They found one in Cairo years ago, chock full of manuscripts, just as this place is."

As they were about to leave, Joseph fished up another jar, the upended bottom of which stuck out beyond the rubbish, and this time he made the greatest find of all. The opening was sealed!

They shook it. Something loose rattled within.

"Golly, this beats everything!" said Michael, examining it.

"We'll certainly take this with us," said Joseph.

It was now four-thirty by Michael's wrist watch, and they reached the cave of bats without incident.

They were halfway across when disaster overtook them!

Moving forward without the aid of the flash, Michael stumbled over a rock and fell forward with a cry of pain.

"My ankle," he moaned. "I've wrenched my ankle."

Joseph knew the accident was a serious one. He deposited his jar carefully on the floor and put his arms round his brother.

"You must lean on me, and we'll try to get out into the passage."

They slowly hobbled across the cave and into the opposite passage for some ten yards, guiding themselves by means of the twine.

Here, by the light of the flash, they looked at the wounded ankle anxiously. It was already badly swollen.

"We had better rest for a bit," said Joseph.

"It's no good staying here," Michael gasped. "We must try to get out."

Joseph had an idea. He made Michael sit on a knapsack with his injured limb off the ground. Then, tying his rope to the strap, he pulled his brother up the slope.

Finally Joseph had to stop. He had been pulling like a horse, and they had not yet covered more than about half

the distance to the entrance.

In the meantime, Sara had returned, out of breath and drenched with sweat, to Aunt Malka's house.

"Michael and Joseph!" she gasped to her father. "They haven't come out from the cave yet."

"We must get help at once," Father said, when he had heard the details. In no time at all several cars had been obtained, and food, blankets, ropes and medical aid had been got together. Manned by a dozen volunteers, the vehicles were soon speeding up the road to the mountains.

When Sara showed them the concealed entrance to the cave, the local residents were amazed. One of their number was a guide who was familiar with all the caves in the district, yet this one was new to him.

"It does not appear in our records at all," he declared, "and if, as the girl says, it goes for a long way underneath, it will have to be examined thoroughly as soon as possible."

Soon the rescue party was arranged. Half a dozen selected men vanished within, bearing, among other things, a stretcher.

Back in the passage Michael and Joseph were resting.

The flash by now had become very weak. They did not talk a great deal, just a few words now and again to keep their spirits up. So you can imagine the astonishment of Joseph, when he heard his brother suddenly cry aloud excitedly, "Something is pulling!"

"What do you mean?" asked Joseph.

"Something is pulling, I tell you! Something is pulling my finger."

Michael had tied the twine round his finger so that he should be able to find it easily in the dark, and now he felt that gentle pulling of Sara who was standing with the others in the outer cave.

"It must be Sara!" he cried. "I'm going to pull also!"

"Michael, Joseph, we're coming!" cried Sara.

In a short while the rescue party had reached them, and Michael was being transferred carefully to the stretcher. Two strong men lifted this, and the return journey was about to begin when—

"Wait!" shouted Joseph, and seizing Sara's flash, he made off down the passage!

He disappeared from sight in a moment, in spite of the frantic cries of his father and sister.

The party waited—there was nothing else they could do—and were relieved to see him return five minutes later. Clutched tightly under his arm was the sealed jar.

Within half an hour the twins were at home and lying in warm beds.

In spite of the lateness of the hour, the full story had of course to be told. The scrap of paper with the copy of the inscription was shown to Father.

"This is a wonderful discovery," he said, "This is a verse from the Torah, and means, 'Behold this is laid up in store with Me, sealed up among My treasures' (Deut. 32:34) . Undoubtedly, the place you saw was a Genizah—"

"I told you so," burst out Michael.

"—and the tablet is a sort of notice to that effect—"

"Oh, please open the jar," begged Joseph.

"—I was going to say that we shall do nothing of the sort. According to your own story, all those scrolls you saw had crumbled to dust. That is because of the effect of the air. Now this jar is sealed. It certainly sounds as though there is a manuscript inside it. We are not going to touch it. Instead, I shall take it along myself tomorrow to the Hebrew University and let them open it."

And that is exactly what he did.

What the University experts found within is now common knowledge. The stir aroused in scholarly circles by the finding of the almost fabulous Book of Jashar was tremendous. Certainly no other archaeological discovery of such significance had been made in this century.

A well-known London newspaper underlined the excitement caused by the news at the time:

"Scholars the world over have been electrified by the news of the discovery in a hitherto unknown cave near Jerusalem of the only known copy of the Book of Jashar.

"Students of the Bible who have studied the Book of Samuel, will remember that the lamentation of David over Saul and Jonathan begins with the words: 'Behold, it is written in the Book of Jashar' (II Samuel, 1:18).

"Works of reference are unanimous, however, in stating that no known copies of the book exist.

"It is to be hoped, therefore, that the public may shortly be in a position to study the Book of Jashar after all.

"The discoverers of both the cave and the manuscripts are two English boys, twins named Goldman, who while on a visit to Israel . . ."

And now what of the twins themselves?

They had of course been praised as never before by all sorts of people, until even they had grown a little bored by it all. Indeed they were quite glad at last when the time came for them to return to England!

Back home, they basked for a time in the glory of their adventure, and might have developed swelled heads, if one of their schoolmates, a youth who had heard the story of their passage through the cave of bats so often that he was thoroughly sick of it, had not had the happy thought of re-naming them the "batty" twins!

After that the subject soon ceased to be discussed in classroom or playground, for the twins knew how to defend their dignity, and by the end of the term, the story—once a nine days' wonder—had been forgotten altogether.

II

The World of
Eastern Europe

Bontshe The Silent

BY ISAAC LOEB PERETZ

DOWN here, in this world, Bontshe the Silent's death made no impression at all. Ask anyone you like who Bontshe was, how he lived, and what he died of, and they won't know.

If a horse had fallen dead in traffic, there would have been more excitement. It would have been mentioned in the papers, and hundreds of people would have crowded round to look at the dead animal—even at the spot where the accident took place.

Bontshe lived quietly and died quietly. He passed through our world like a shadow.

No wine was drunk at Bontshe's circumcision, and he made no beautiful speech at his Bar Mitzvah. He lived like a little grain of sand on the seashore, among millions of his kind; and when the wind lifted him and blew him over to the other side of the sea, nobody noticed it.

When he was alive, the mud in the street preserved no impression on his feet; after his death, the wind overturned the little wooden marker on his grave.

A quiet birth, a quiet life, a quiet death, and a quieter burial.

But it was not so in the other world. There Bontshe's death made a great impression. The biggest angels with the broadest wings flew about and told one another: "Bontshe the Silent is to take his seat in the Heavenly Academy!" In Paradise there was a noise and a joyful tumult: "Bontshe the Silent!"

Very young angels with diamond eyes, golden-threaded wings, and silver slippers ran delightedly to meet him. The rustle of the wings, the tap-tap of the little slippers, and the merry laughter of the fresh, rosy mouths, filled all the heavens and reached to the Throne of Glory, and God Himself knew that Bontshe the Silent was coming.

Abraham, of the Bible, stood in the gate, his right hand stretched out with a hearty greeting, and a sweet smile lit up his old face.

What were they bringing through heaven?

Two angels were pushing a gold armchair into Paradise for Bontshe the Silent.

What flashed so brightly?

They were carrying a gold crown set with precious stones —all for Bontshe the Silent.

"Before the decision of the Heavenly Court has been given?" everyone asked.

"Oh," replied the angels, "that will be a mere formality. Even the prosecutor won't say a word against Bontshe the Silent. The case will not last five minutes."

Bontshe was beside himself with terror, and he never heard the president call out: "The case of Bontshe!" adding, as he handed the deeds to the lawyer for Bontshe, "Read, but make haste!"

The whole hall went round and round in Bontshe's eyes; there was a rushing in his ears. And through the rushing he heard more and more clearly the voice of the lawyer, speaking sweetly as a violin.

"His name," he heard, "fitted him perfectly. He never was heard to complain of either God or man; there was never a flash of hatred in his eye."

Still Bontshe did not understand, and a hard voice, the voice of the prosecutor, interrupted: "No speeches, please!"

"He kept silent," the defense attorney went on, "even when his mother died, and his father seized him by the hair in a fit of drunkenness, and flung him out into the street on a snowy winter night. He quietly picked himself up out of

the snow and ran wherever his feet carried him.

"He kept silent all the way—however hungry he might be, he only begged with his eyes. He looked about for the hardest work, and kept silent.

"Once," continued the lawyer, after a sip of water, "a change entered his life: a carriage on rubber tires came flying along, drawn by two runaway horses. The driver lay some distance off on the pavement with a cracked skull. The terrified horses foamed at the mouth, sparks shot from their hoofs, their eyes shone like fiery lamps on a winter night, and in the carriage, more dead than alive, sat a man.

"And Bontshe stopped the horses. And the man he had saved was a charitable Jew, who was not ungrateful.

"He put the dead man's whip into Bontshe's hands and Bontshe became a coachman. More than that—he was provided with a wife, and later on—with a child."

"Me, they mean me!" Bontshe assured himself again, and yet he had not the courage to give a glance at the Heavenly Court.

Illustrated by E. Schloss

"He kept silent when his wife ran away from him, leaving him with the child.

"He was also silent fifteen years later, when the child had grown up and was strong enough to throw him out of the house.

"He kept silent even in the hospital after he was run over by the same man whose life he had saved.

"He kept silent when the doctor would not come to his bedside without being paid fifteen kopeks, and when the attendant demanded another five—for changing his linen."

Once more Bontshe trembled all over; he knew that after the defense attorney comes the prosecutor. Who knows what he will say?

"Gentlemen," began the prosecutor, in a voice biting and acid as vinegar—but he broke off.

"Gentlemen," he began again, and his voice was milder. "Gentlemen! He was silent! I will be silent, too!"

There was a hush—then the sound of a new, soft, trembling voice:

"Bontshe, my child," it spoke like a harp, "my dear child Bontshe!"

And Bontshe's heart melted within him. Now he wished to lift up his eyes, but they were blinded with tears; he had never felt this way before. "My child! My Bontshe!"—no one, since his mother died, had spoken to him such soft words in such a voice.

"My child," continued the presiding judge, "you have suffered and kept silent; there is no whole limb, no whole bone in your body, without a scar, without a wound, not a fiber of your soul that has not bled—and you kept silent.

"There they did not understand. Perhaps you yourself did not know that you might have cried out, and that at your cry the walls of Jericho would have shaken and fallen. You yourself knew nothing of your hidden power.

"In the other world your silence was not understood, but this is the world of truth; here you will receive your reward.

"The Heavenly Court will not judge you; the Heavenly Court will not pass sentence upon you. Take what you will! Everything is yours!"

Bontshe looked up for the first time. He was dazzled; everything shined and flashed and streamed with light.

"Really?" he asked shyly.

"Yes, really!" answered the presiding judge firmly. "I tell you, everything is yours; everything in heaven belongs to you. Because all that shines and sparkles is only the reflection of your soul. You only take of what is yours."

"Really?" asked Bontshe again, this time in a firmer voice.

"Really! Really! Really!" they answered him from all sides.

"Well, if it is so," Bontshe smiled, "I would like to have every day, for breakfast, a hot roll with fresh butter."

The Court and the angels dropped their heads, ashamed; while the prosecutor burst out into loud laughter.

The Short Friday

BY HAYIM NAHMAN BIALIK

IF THOSE who are up and doing their chores on ordinary Fridays deserve praise, those who are up and doing their chores on the shortest Friday of the year deserve it far more. As you know, you must not be lazy on the Short Friday or you will violate the Sabbath.

So Rabbi Lippe, who lived in a small village in Russia, began to take steps against the Short Friday long before daylight. He treated himself with the greatest strictness, for if he would be even a little bit late, the entire order of his day would be spoiled.

Now what was it that Rabbi Lippe had to do that took up so much time? Well, first there were the preliminary prayers. Then came the Psalms to say, and then the main prayers, followed by a few chapters to study, a lesson in Talmud, and finally, the Bible portion of the week.

At noon began a fresh series of tasks. First he had to bathe, then trim his nails, then prepare snuff for the Sabbath. Sometimes he was called upon to make a decision on a question of Jewish law. And what with one thing and another, the day would be gone.

So it is not at all surprising that Rabbi Lippe rose on the Short Friday together with the morning star. Ah, but what happens to the best-laid plans of mice and men . . . ?

Rabbi Lippe had finished all the early morning tasks on this particular Short Friday, when the door opened and a peasant walked in. The stranger rested his whip against the doorpost, took off his heavy gloves, put his hand into his coat and handed the rabbi a letter. The rabbi read the letter and shrugged. An interruption of his schedule on the Short Friday, of all times!

The wealthy Mr. Getzi, the rich farmer of the neighboring village, was inviting him to be present at a *brit milah*—a circumcision ceremony—for his first grandson. The sleigh was waiting to take the rabbi to the neighboring village. Mr. Getzi had sent along three items to encourage Rabbi Lippe to come. One was three rubles, the second was a huge sack of potatoes and a goose, and the third was a fur overcoat and felt overshoes so that the rabbi might wrap himself up well and keep properly warm.

"So what's to be done?" sighed Rabbi Lippe. He dressed himself, kissed the mezuzah on the doorpost, climbed into the sleigh, and away they went.

The road was good and within an hour the rabbi reached the house of Mr. Getzi.

The company had already come. The guests finished their prayers. Then the men passed the baby from hand to hand, so that everyone could admire him. Rabbi Lippe, who was to be the godfather, put the infant on his lap and blessed him. And then a feast began. There was fish, and meat, and roast goose, and pudding with raisins. There was also brandy to drink. This brandy had been stored in Mr. Getzi's cellar for years and was very old and very good. The rabbi drank one glass and then one more. It made him sleepy.

Outside, the coachman, Ivan, was also having his share of the food. He also had one, two, three, four glasses of brandy.

He was even sleepier than the rabbi.

The rabbi realized he had to get back home before sundown, so he arose and said farewell to his host, and all of a sudden he heard the clock strike three. He jumped up, put all his heavy winter clothing on, went outside, awoke Ivan and climbed into the sleigh. Ivan whipped the horse and off they went.

The cold air and the motion of the sleigh, together with the fact that he had awakened so early this short Friday, put the rabbi to sleep. Ivan, who had had too much to drink, also fell asleep. So the horse went whichever way he wished. Instead of taking the road the horse decided to go right out over the fields. The snow began falling and the horse could not see where he was running and bumped into a wall. The sleigh turned over. Rabbi Lippe and Ivan woke up and found themselves in darkness covered with snow.

"Oh, what a terrible thing! On the Sabbath!" The rabbi's heart was heavy and he wept. Ivan set the sleigh aright, but the rabbi did not want to get in. He did not want to ride on the Sabbath. But when he looked around and saw only forest and darkness, snow and cold, and heard the wolves howling, he became afraid. He climbed back in the sleigh and they drove on. Ivan could not see where he was going in the dark and at last, about midnight, they reached an inn. The rabbi noticed that the burned-out Sabbath candles were on the table, and the tablecloth was covered with crumbs from the Sabbath dinner. He did not want to disturb the innkeeper and so he sat down on a bench. Finally his beard and hair thawed out, for they had been frozen solid. He prayed to God over and over to forgive him and then stretched out on a bench and fell asleep. Ivan went into the kitchen and slept on the floor.

The cock crowed. The innkeeper, Feivka was his name,

awoke. He jumped up, put on his clothes, and went out into the big room to see who had arrived at his inn during the night. He was amazed to see Rabbi Lippe sleeping on the bench.

"It cannot be," reasoned Feivka, "that Rabbi Lippe would travel on the Sabbath. I must have made a mistake about the days of the week. Tomorrow the whole village will know about it."

As soon as he reached this conclusion, he dashed off to remove all signs of the Sabbath before the rabbi awoke. He put away the candlesticks, the remains of the Sabbath meals, and the white tablecloth. Then he awoke his wife and daughter and told them to clear away any remaining signs of the Sabbath. In a few moments the house looked as though it were a weekday. A fire burned, the teakettle bur-

Illustrated by Bill Giacalone

bled, a hammer banged, and an axe chopped. Feivka himself was kneading dough and his daughter was peeling potatoes into a pot.

The rabbi slept. Feivka said his morning prayers out loud, watching the rabbi out of the corner of his eye. At last Rabbi Lippe awoke, full of aches and pains. Where was he? And where was the Sabbath? Peasants were at the inn, a samovar was boiling, hammers and axes were pounding. The rabbi was ashamed. "I must have slept straight through the Sabbath," he thought. He prayed, "Lord of the universe, please forgive me." He arose and dressed quickly, summoned Ivan and said farewell to Feivka. Then they sped away. The sleigh just flew over the hard icy ground and now that it was daylight Ivan had no trouble knowing just which way to go.

And at the noon hour, when the congregation had left the synagogue and, in all the glory of the Sabbath, was returning home, and when everybody was wishing everybody else a good Sabbath, in that moment there sped toward them from the outskirts a speedy sleigh. And in that selfsame sleigh—sat none other than Rabbi Lippe!

Adapted from the original by Bea Stadtler

Three Little Heads

BY SHOLOM ALEICHEM

I OFFER you a present for Shavuot, a picture of three little heads, three wonderfully fine heads of poor, tattered, barefoot children. All three little heads are dark, with curly hair and eyes big and bright that stare at you with wonder and always seem to ask the question: "Why?"

The three little heads—Avremchik, Moisechik and Dvora —are two bothers and their little sister. Avremchik and Moisechik— that was what their father, Peiseh the box-maker, called them. Peiseh the boxmaker stands on his feet all day and cuts cardboard and puts together boxes, and sings songs, some of the old ones and some new ones, some Jewish and some not a bit Jewish—many of them not a bit Jewish—happy sad songs with a sad happy tune.

The three—Avremchik, Moisechik and Dvorka—were born and grew up in the same place, between the wall and the oven in a single crowded room. Every day the three saw the same things before them: their jolly father who cut the cardboard, pasted boxes and sang songs; and their worried mother, who cooked and baked, swept and scrubbed, and was never finished.

One window, that's all there was. One small window. The three little heads try to reach the one small window—and what can they see there? A wall, a high, broad, gray, damp wall, always damp, always dripping, even in summer. Does the sun ever come in here at all? Of course the sun comes in —sometimes. That is, not the sun itself, but a glimmering reflection of the sun. And when that happens it is time for rejoicing. The three little heads crowd against the small window, look up, way up, and glimpse a long, narrow, blue strip, like a long blue ribbon.

"There, do you see that, children? That's the sky!"

That is Avremchik speaking. Avremchik knows. Avremchik goes to heder. He is already studying the alphabet. The heder is not so far—two houses away, or rather two doors away. Oh, what stories Avremchik tells about heder. For instance, Avremchik knows that a tree grows. Of course he himself has never seen a tree grow any more than they have—there are no trees on their street—but he knows (he heard it in heder) that trees bear fruit. And that is why when you eat fruit you say, "Blessed art Thou, O Lord our God, King of the universe, Who createst the fruit of the tree." Avremchik knows everything! but he doesn't know how or in what manner these things grow either. For on their street there is no field, no garden, there are no trees, there's not a blade of grass—not one! On their street there are only tall buildings, gray walls, high chimneys pouring smoke, and every building is covered with window panes, thousands of little windowpanes, and inside the buildings are machines that run by themselves, and carts that are moved without horses. And aside from that there is nothing, nothing.

Even a bird is rarely seen. Sometimes a sparrow blunders into the neighborhood, and the sparrow is as gray as the walls themselves. It pecks once or twice at the cobblestones, rises and flies away. And chickens, ducks, geese? Once in a great while they have a quarter of a chicken for Saturday, chicken with a pale scrawny leg. How many legs does a chicken have? Obviously four. Just like a horse. That is Avremchik's opinion, and Avremchik knows everything.

Born and brought up in the great city, in the large buildings, in crowded quarters, the three children never had a chance to see anything alive—a hen, a cow, or any other creature except a cat. They have their own cat, a live one, a large cat, gray as the tall, gray, damp walls. The cat is their one joy. They play with it whenever they can. They tie a kerchief around its head and call it auntie, and laugh uproariously.

But then their mother catches them at it and goes after them, slaps one's hands, boxes another's ears, sends them back to their place behind the oven. The eldest, Avremchik, begins to talk and the younger ones listen, look up wide-

eyed at their older brother and listen. Avremchik says that
their mother is right. He says that you're not supposed to
play with a cat, because a cat is an unclean thing, an evil
spirit. Avremchik knows everything, everything. Is there
anything in the world that he doesn't know?

Avremchik tells them all these things, and the children's
eyes sparkle and they envy their brother, who knows everything—even what happens in heaven. Avremchik swears
that twice a year—one night of Sukkot and one night of Shavuot—the skies split open. Of course he has never seen the

Illustrated by Lili Cassel Wronker

skies split open, because where they live you can't see the sky. But some of his schoolmates saw it happen. They swore that they saw it. And they wouldn't swear to a lie, would they?

Now they wait for their father to come home. Their father has gone to the market with a stack of boxes.

"Children, what do you think he's going to bring us today?"

And the children begin to guess. They count on their fingers—everything that could possibly be at the market, everything that the eye could see and the heart could long for—all those oddly shaped buns and the beigel and the candy. But none of them guessed right, and I am afraid that none of you will guess it either. This time Peiseh the box-maker brought neither buns nor beigel nor candy. He brought grasses, a bagful of grasses, strange long, green, sweet-smelling grasses.

And the three little heads, Avremchik, Moisechek and Dvorka, surrounded their father.

"Oh, what is it? What did you bring? What is it?"

"Greens. Can't you see?"

"What do you mean—greens?"

"Greens for the holidays. It's Shavuot tonight. All the Jews need greens for Shavuot."

"Where do you get them?"

"Where do you get them? M—m—m . . . You buy them at the market."

And saying this, he scatters the green fragrant grass over the freshly swept floor. He keeps some of it in his hands and fingers it and sniffs at it joyfully.

"Isn't it wonderful?"

"Wonderful for you!" says their mother. "A wonderful litter. Something new for the children to mess with."

That's how their mother is, as she goes on with her work, always worried, always burdened, just the opposite of their father.

And the three little heads look at their mother, look at their father, look at each other. And when their parents' backs are turned for a moment, they throw themselves on the floor, bury their heads in the fragrant grasses, fondle and kiss the rough blades that are called greens, and that Jews must have for their holidays, and that you buy at the market.

Everything can be found at the market, even greens. Their father brings them everything. There are so many things that Jews must have, and they get them. Even greens . . . Even greens . . .

The Sabbath Journey

BY DAVID EINHORN

"TAKE the chestnut mare from the stable and bring her to the meadow. Why shouldn't she enjoy an Oneg Shabbat too? She worked hard enough all week long."

Father had only to say this once to Elia. No sooner had the family finished its Sabbath dinner and said grace than Elia ran to the stable.

Elia's father was a wagon-driver in a Jewish townlet of eastern Europe. The chestnut mare was practically a member of the family, because without her there would be no way of making a living.

Elia, just thirteen and still studying in the heder, was the mare's best friend. The family used to say that Chestnut and Elia had a secret language all their own.

On summer Sabbaths Elia had the privilege of leading Chestnut out to the meadow where the "Jewish" horses would graze all day long, free from bit and harness.

Entering the stable, Elia found Chestnut eagerly waiting, one ear cocked, the other flattened against her head, and her large, black, moist eyes fixed lovingly on him.

"Good Sabbath, Chestnut," said Elia. The mare raised her head and together they left the stable. Elia led the way, hands clasped behind him, and Chestnut followed carefully, step by step.

The townlet seemed deserted in the hot Sabbath sun; no living soul was to be seen and all the stores were shut tight. The only sound was the quiet chanting of the Sabbath *zemirot* wafting through the open windows of the little houses where people still sat over the noonday meal. Peace reigned everywhere; it was as if all of Nature was observing the Sabbath.

In the meadow the wagon-drivers were already lolling on the green grass, their arms under their heads, their faces turned to the heavens, sound asleep. Their horses stood with half-closed eyes, lazily tugging at the grass, swatting flies with their tails, now and then taking a little nap standing up.

Elia stretched out, his fists clenched behind his head, and studied the small sunlit clouds wandering aimlessly in the blue sky. A shower of sharp notes, like tiny crystal bells ringing, filled the air.

They say that those are skylarks singing, but I don't see a single bird. Maybe they're in those golden clouds. And Elia closed his eyes.

Suddenly a warm breath carressed his face and something cool and moist pressed his c h e e k . Elia looked up. It was Chestnut.

"Sh-sh-sh," Chestnut said in a human voice. "Don't wake

them up. Come on, let's take a Sabbath stroll."

"Chestnut," cried Elia, "you've been bewitched! Whoever heard of a talking horse?"

"Sh . . . sh . . . be quiet," Chestnut whispered. "Shame on you. You've studied the Bible. Don't you remember that Balaam's donkey once spoke?"

"Well, aren't you the smart one! Where did you learn all that?"

"We animals speak very seldom, so we hear a great deal. And when a person listens more than he talks, he can learn a whole lot. Now climb on my back and we'll take a Sabbath stroll."

"Chestnut, you know I'm not allowed to ride on you on the Sabbath!"

"True, but that is only if you saddle and harness me and hold a whip in your hand. But this time I am inviting you. That's just like boys playing horse and climbing on each other's shoulders. That's permitted on the Sabbath."

"But someone will see us."

"No one will see us, Elia."

"How far will you take me?"

"Very far."

"But one isn't allowed to go too far on the Sabbath."

"True, Elia. But we won't go too far on the Sabbath."

"That's impossible!"

"Oh, it is possible, Elia. Just yesterday you were thinking how much you missed your brother, Moshe, the one who's in America. So you dreamt about America. Now tell me, were you in New York or did New York come to you? . . . Hurry up now, Elia. Up on my back!"

Elia suddenly beheld cities, countries, rivers, mountains, seas, fields dressed in summer green; now it was autumn, winter, spring—everything zoomed by with fantastic speed.

Then Elia spied a wonderful, many-colored castle. A vast garden, gleaming with the light of seven suns, lay behind the gates. Elia and Chestnut entered the garden.

They found themselves among graceful trees, heavy with sweet fruit, and singing birds decked with gay feathers. Grazing on the lea were wolves and sheep, tigers and gazelles, lions and buffalo, foxes and rabbits. Quietly, peacefully, they munched the grass and nibbled the fruit that fell from the trees.

"Where are we?" Elia asked Chestnut.

"This is the first Sabbath in the Garden of Eden. Just after God created the world and every living thing in six days."

"I know," Elia said. "That was when peace ruled, before Adam disobeyed God and was banished from the Garden of Eden. My father says that after that man always had to work hard, without even an hour of peace."

"Hold tight," Chestnut said. "We're taking off!" And mountains, oceans and continents swiftly raced by Elia. All at once his eye was caught by a broad river and barges bearing square blocks of sandstone. Thousands of half-naked people towed the barges with ropes to the river bank. They piled the hewn stone on platforms resting on round wooden poles and thousands of other workers drew the stones to a gigantic triangular structure.

"Say," Elia exclaimed, "we're in Egypt and those are the Israelites!"

One group of men sat in the hot sun eating c r u s t s of bread.

"Just one free day a week!" a worker moaned. "One free day to rest and see my family. Sun-up to sundown, it's work and sweat till we wait for death to free us."

"Just one free day a week!" the others echoed. "Free from

work, from slavery, from the whip."

"We want a day of rest for everyone," a man cried out, "not just for human beings! For cattle, too, and for horses, and for all who work for men."

"That's the first time anybody ever mentioned us," Chestnut said softly. "It's time somebody realized that we need rest as much as people do."

In a trice, a mountain loomed close. It was enveloped in flames and smoke and a thick mass of people surrounded it. From the mountain, accompanied by thunder and lightning, a mighty voice called out.

"Remember the Sabbath day to keep it holy. Six days shall you labor, but the seventh is a day of rest for the Lord your God. In it you shall do no manner of work, neither you nor your son nor your daughter nor your manservant, nor your maidservant, nor your cattle, nor the stranger within your gates. For in six days the Lord made heaven and earth, the

Illustrated by E. Schloss

sea, and all that is in them. And He rested on the seventh day; therefore the Lord blessed the Sabbath day, and made it holy!"

Elia heard the thunder rumbling among the hills. He reached for Chestnut, frightened. "Chestnut!" he cried. "Chestnut!" Elia opened his eyes, rubbed them, and looked around. The sun was beginning to set. In the distance, a gray thundercloud released flashes of summer lighting.

Chestnut lay nearby, gazing at Elia, a smile in her large black eyes.

Elia saw his father on the little bridge that spanned the stream.

"Elia! You've slept quite well, haven't you? I see you've forgotten that it is time to eat *shalosh se'udot,* the third Sabbath meal. Everyone's waiting for you!"

Elia scrambled to his feet. The wagon-drivers and their horses were gone. Only he and Chestnut were left. Chestnut rested her head on Elia's shoulder.

"Don't be afraid, Chestnut," Elia whispered in her ear. "This will remain our secret forever. I'll never tell a soul."

Translated from the Yiddish by Morris Epstein

My Brother Eli's Drink

BY SHOLOM ALEICHEM

I'M TERRIBLY BUSY. I'm earning money. I'm selling a drink which my brother Eli makes all by himself. He learned how to make it out of a book which costs only one ruble and which can teach you to earn one hundred rubles a month and over. As soon as my brother discovered that such a book existed in the wide world, he sent the ruble—his very last ruble—and told mother she need not worry any longer.

At last, the book is here. No sooner did we unpack it than my brother Eli sat down to read it. Goodness, what didn't he read out of the book! So many methods for making money by all sorts of recipes! A recipe for making one hundred rubles a month by preparing first-class ink. A recipe for making one hundred rubles a month by making shoeblacking. A recipe for making one hundred rubles a month by preparing liqueurs, sweet brandies, lemonade, soda water, cider and other drinks . . .

My brother Eli decided upon the last recipe. First, be-

Illustrated by E. Schloss

cause with this one, one can earn more than a hundred rubles a month. Secondly, cider's a drink which costs little and sells well. Particularly during a hot summer as this.

The cider which my brother Eli makes from the recipe is a special kind of drink. Just how it's made I cannot tell you. My brother Eli doesn't let anyone come near him when he's working. We only see him pour the water in.But when he's really making the cider he shuts himself up in mother's room. Neither Mother, his wife, nor I am allowed in. But if you promise to keep it a secret, I can tell you there is more water in it than anything else. The more water, the more cider. All this is mixed together with an ordinary stick— that's what it tells you to do in the book—and the drink is ready. Then you pour it into a large pitcher and you throw in a piece of ice. Without ice, cider is good for nothing. I needn't tell you why. Once I tasted cider without ice and I thought I'd expire . . .

When the first barrel of cider was ready it was decided that the one to sell it on the streets would be I. Who else but me? I was delighted when I heard the news. My brother Eli started to teach me how to do it. With one hand I had to hold the pitcher by a rope, with the other a glass, and in order to attract attention, I had to sing out loud,

"Jews, here's a drink!
 A glass costs a penny!
Sweet, nice and cold!
 And don't drink too many!"
As I mentioned before, my voice is a good one—a soprano, inherited from my father, may he rest in peace. I started singing and turned the song inside out:
"You can't drink too many!
 Drink, here's a glass!
 A Jew costs a penny!
 Sweet, nice and cold!"
I don't know whether it was because they liked my singing, or because the drink was really so good, or because the day was so hot, but I sold the first pitcher in half an hour

and came home with three-quarters of a ruble. My brother Eli gave the money to Mother and another pitcherful to me. He said if I could do this five or six times a day, we'd earn exactly one hundred rubles a month. Figure it out for yourselves. Omitting the four Sabbaths in a month, and counting the original cost of the drink, what would be the percentage we'd make on it? The drink costs us almost nothing. All the money goes into ice. Therefore, you've got to try to sell the cider so quickly that the ice lasts for the second pitcher, the

third, and so on. To do it quickly enough you've got to go
fast. As a matter of fact, you've got to run. And after me
runs a whole crowd of kids. They mimic my singing. But
they can't disconcert me. I get my pitcherful sold rapidly
and run home to fetch more.

I don't know myself how much I made on the first day.
All I know is that my brother, his wife, and my mother
praised me to the skies. For supper they gave me a slice of
cantaloupe, a slice of watermelon, and two prunes. As to
cider, I hardly need mention it. We drink cider as if it were
water . . . When it's time to go to sleep, Mother arranges my
bed on the floor and asks me whether my feet hurt. My
brother Eli laughs at her. He says, "I'm the kind of boy
whom nothing hurts."

"Certainly!" I say. "Give me a pitcher and I"ll go sell
cider in the middle of the night!"

Everybody laughs at my boast, but in Mother's eyes I see
tears. That's an old story: a mother's got to cry. What I'd
like to know is whether all mothers cry all the time, like
mine?

Our business has been going on swimmingly. Each day is
hotter than the last. It sizzles. People wilt with the heat,
children like flies. If not for a glass of cider, they'd all burn
to a cinder. Ten times a day I return with the pitcher and
with money. My brother squints into the barrel and sees
that there is little left. He hits upon a bright idea and pours
in more water. But I had discovered this bright idea before
he did. I must confess I've done the trick several times.

Who would ever guess that such a thing could happen to
us, and that our drink would become as worthless as a straw?
Might as well pour it into the slop pail . . . At least, thank
God, I wasn't arrested . . .

Listen to this: one day I took the cider to our neighbor

Pessie. Everyone took a glassful. Me, too. Figuring that I was short twelve or thirteen glasses, I went into the room where they keep water. But instead of the water barrel, I evidently hit upon the barrel where they wash clothes and filled my pitcher with twelve or thirteen glasses of soapsuds. I went out into the street.

A man stops me, pays me a penny and orders a glass. He gulps it down and makes a grimace.

"Boy, what sort of drink is this?"

I pay no attention to him. There are two others waiting for me to pour. One of them drinks half a glass, The other a third of a glass. They pay, spit and walk away. Another man takes a glass to his lips, sips it and remarks that it smells of soap and has a salty taste. A fourth looks at the glass and hands it back to me.

"What have you got there?"

"A drink."

"A drink? That's a stink, not a drink!"

Spying a crowd, a policeman comes up and asks what's the matter. They tell him. He looks into the pitcher and orders a drink. I pour out a glassful for him. He takes a sip, spits it out and becomes purple in the face.

"Where did you get these soapsuds?" he demands.

"Out of a book," I say. "My brother makes it all by himself."

"Who is your brother?" he asks me.

"My brother Eli," I answer.

The policeman holds me by the hand and wants to take us —that is, me and the cider—to the police station. The noise increases. "He's an orphan! Spare the orphan!" I hear from all sides . . . My heart tells me that I'm in a mess. I look around, "Jews, help me out!" Somebody wants to give the policeman a bribe. The policeman refuses it. An old man, with sly eyes, suddenly calls out to me in Hebrew.

"Youth! Remove thy hand from the watchman's, lift thy limbs and show him the soles of thy feet!"

I tear my hand from the policeman's, lift my limbs, and show him the soles of my feet . . . More dead than alive I burst into our house.

"Where is the pitcher?" asks my brother Eli.

"In the police station!" I reply and fall weeping into Mother's arms.

Our House of Prayer

BY DAVID EINHORN

IN THE days when hundreds of Jewish villages and town-lets dotted the endless plains of White Russia, it often happened that a tired Jewish traveler raised his eyes from the dusty road and saw a building with a triple, pagoda-like roof on the horizon.

It was the village synagogue.

The traveler thankfully glanced heavenward, heaved a sigh of relief, and sat down to rest on the nearest rock.

The synagogue, majestically silhouetted against the blue sky, had reassured him that a brotherly reception, including a warm meal and a bed on which to stretch his weary limbs, would soon be his.

When he entered the village, there was no need to ask for an address—the house of prayer, which was at least three hundred years old, towered above the squat houses with their wooden or straw roofs and served as a friendly guide, beckoning the stranger to the courtyard of the synagogue in the center of the village.

The synagogue occupied the center of this large area. It had four high walls of stout cedar topped with a triple roof; but from the inside the walls appeared much higher, because one quarter of the synagogue was built below ground and a steep flight of steps had to be descended to reach the floor.

Illustrated by Lazlo Matulay

119

There was a reason for this. According to tradition, when the community suffered deep sorrow and the inhabitants gathered in the synagogue to pray, their prayers would go up to heaven from the depths of the earth. As King David said in Psalm 130; "Out of the depths have I called Thee, O Lord."

In contrast to the low surrounding houses, the square synagogue stood out like a noble palace. The high walls were ornamented with colorful paintings of fantastic trees and flowers. Woven among them were drawings of the musical instruments upon which the Levites had played in the Temple. The most breathtaking side was the east, or mizrah section, where over the Ark was fashioned a huge frame carved through and through with branches and flowers, birds and deer, lions and leopards. The bimah, where the Torah was read, was in the center of the synagogue. Over it spread a canopy carved with leaves and fruits. In the center of the canopy hung the Eternal Light—the Ner Tamid.

For the children, there were two sections on both sides of the rear entrance. The sections consisted of several rows of benches, each a little higher than the one in front. Every seat had a carved design—a lion, a tree, or a flower, copied from the Ark or from the walls around. On Rosh Hashanah and Yom Kippur, the children sat on these benches under the watchful eyes of the teachers.

For us children, the synagogue was a building of mystery, wrapped in many old legends. In summer evenings, when the last rays of the setting sun filtered through the colored window panes and filled the synagogue with rainbow-hued shafts of light, we would tremblingly descend into the quiet house of prayer and listen to the echoes from the outside. How eerie they sounded! We would never stay too long. When the sun went down and shadows stole across the syna-

gogue floor and the Ner Tamid suddenly blazed forth with flaming brightness, we tumbled outside to sit on the stone steps and exchanged strange and wonderful stories that our parents had told us.

The synagogue courtyard hummed with activity. All around the courtyard were buildings, most of them with brick or stone walls—each of them was called a *Bet Ha-Midrash,* or House of Study. During the warm summer evenings all the windows were wide open. Light streamed through them, and voices mingled in a rich flood of chant and debate. There was the still, almost sad singsong of the yeshiva students, bent over the fine print of their Talmud. From a second building streamed an excited discussion between two old scholars on a point of Jewish law, or about a biblical quotation. From a third set of windows came a heated sermon on the good way of life, delivered by a wandering maggid, or preacher, or perhaps the calm voice of a rabbi studying the wisdom of the Bible and the teachings of the great Jewish sages with a group of tradesmen. Outside, small groups gathered about the open doors, commenting on world news they had read in the three or four Yiddish newspapers which passed from one neighbor to another in the village.

The House of Study was actually a community center for

the Jewish citizens. In the Bet Ha-Midrash they studied, prayed, worried over their problems, and thus spent their few free hours. In the east end were the Holy Ark and the Torah scrolls. The opposite wall was lined with holy books —*s'farim*—which were free for all to use.

Each *Bet Ha-Midrash* had its own personality, depending on who were its regular "customers." Every craft had its own House of Study. There was no village without a "tailors' *Bet Ha-Midrash*" and a "shoemakers' *Bet Ha-midrash*." Sometimes several trades joined hands to support a single House of Study. Each had its own teacher, who in the evenings studied Mishnah or Bible with his tradesmen.

On cold winter nights everyone gathered around the big stove. The wayward traveler, passing through the village, joined the group. There the shamash sought him out and, after a friendly *Shalom Aleikhem,* inquired whether he knew anyone in the village or was just passing through. If the man was a stranger, the shamash arranged lodging in the *Hakhnasat Orkhim* (the house for the wayfarer), and saw that a place was set for him at some citizen's table.

Late at night most of the windows grew dark. The citizens returned to their homes. Here and there, perhaps, a lamp still burned and a yeshiva student swayed over his *shtender,* or high desk, his face almost lost in the large Talmud; softly he chanted a sad strain that had been used in Talmud study for generations before him.

It was then that the sky, filled with twinkling stars, seemed to come closer to the quiet village, and the silhouette of the old synagogue stretched ever higher, until bathed in pale starlight, the synagogue took up its faithful watch over the little community that held it so dear to its heart.

Translated from the Yiddish by Morris Epstein

'Wear Them in Good Health'

BY DAVID FRISCHMAN

THE tailor was very poor. His son was still a child, with a pale-white face and black glowing eyes.

The last three nights before Pesah, the tailor had not slept a wink. Day and night he was bent over his workbench making clothes for the wealthy banker, for his sons and sons-in-law, and for their children. The very afternoon before the Seder he had been hard at work until the shadows began to lengthen. Only then did he get up from his seat, gather up the newly made clothes and deliver them to their owners.

The wealthy banker, his sons-in-law, and their children dressed themselves in the new suits and coats and came to synagogue for the evening services. The tailor also came to the synagogue, but he had no new suit on. He had only washed his face hurriedly. Neither did his little son put on a new suit. He too had only washed his face before joining his father at the services.

In the synagogue, full of light and joy and peace this evening, the tailor was so exhausted that he could hardly keep awake. Faintly he heard the chanting of the hazzan, the rustle of new silk and the swish of the new linings of the clothes he had fashioned with his own hands. His little son also heard the rustle of the silk and the swish of the linings and his face became paler and his black eyes burned brighter.

Later, at the Seder in his dingy attic, peace and rest came to the tailor. Was it not Yom Tov? The little room had been swept clean of all scraps of cloth. The table was set with the Seder plate and wine cups. He was "king" this night. On his right sat the "queen" and on his left the "prince."

The prince, his son, asked the Four Questions. His. pale face flushed and his burning eyes became blurred, for he was not accustomed to the letters of the Haggadah.

The father, like all fathers on this night, read the answers —stories about slavery and freedom and about wise men who sat up all night telling the Passover stories. The boy listened, although he did not understand a word.

Suddenly, he stopped his father and he asked another question. This time it was a new question—not one from the Haggadah. "Father! Why did no one say 'Tis-hadesh' to me? All the boys in the synagogue said 'Tis-hadesh' to each other, but not to me." His pale face grew paler and his black eyes glowed like live coals.

The poor boy's father did not know what to answer. There was nothing about this in the Haggadah.

"My son," he said at last, "one who has no new clothes is not told 'Tis-hadesh.' "

"But why don't I have a new suit? No one has ever, ever said 'Tis-hadesh' to me."

His mother sat across the table. Their eyes met; hers were tearful, his were glowing torches. "With God's will, next year," his mother answered, "next year you will have a new suit for Pesah." And she kissed him tenderly on his forehead. The boy sat there, and his eyes were the eyes of a dreamer waiting for a hope to come true.

When Passover came next year, there was no new suit for the boy. Kisses, warm and tender—these his mother could give him, but not a new suit.

Another year passed by, and another, and still another. The lad still wore his old suit. And he always asked: "Why?" He felt neither envy nor jealousy, only pain. When he was at school and saw all the other boys in their suits, which only a day, or a week, or a month ago had been new,

he did not envy them. He only felt a pain in his heart. The new clothes he saw in the streets and in the shop windows sharpened his pain. Not even hunger pained him as much as this one thought which filled his whole little being. It was a longing, longing for the word "Tis-hadesh."

Only once was he happy. It was at night. When he awoke in tears and his mother asked him why he had been crying, he told her that just a few moments ago his friends had been there. Each one touched his new suit and each one said to him, "Tis-hadesh, Tis-hadesh!" He was so happy, but now all was gone.

The lad became a day-dreamer, dreaming always of the word "Tis-hadesh." During his sleep, however, that dream never repeated itself again. And he still waited to hear the magic word "Tis-hadesh" said to him.

The child grew up and became a boy. At twelve, he went to work as a tailor's apprentice. And still he had no new

Illustrated by Bill Giacalone

clothes. The tailor for whom he worked beat him, and the other assistants pinched his skin where it showed through the rags he wore. But none of these insults and pranks hurt him. Only when he got hold of a needle and thread and began working on a new coat did he feel a pain in his heart. The coat, not the needle, hurt him. At such times his face grew pale, his eyes glowed, and his ears would buzz with the sound of "Tis-hadesh."

When the tailor sent him to deliver new clothes to the homes of the rich and he saw all the wealth and beauty there, and then when he returned to his room and beheld how poor and bare it was—even then he remembered only one thing: that they had new clothes and he had none.

What sin had he committed not to be worthy of a new coat? What good deeds had they done that they should have new clothes?

Three years passed, and then three more. He was a young man of eighteen. And no one had ever yet said "Tis-hadesh" to him. His face was very, very white now. He coughed frequently, occasionally coughing up blood. But his eyes still glowed like live coals. His very soul was afire. His whole being, his very brain was nothing but one great longing—longing for the sound of Tis-hadesh. Why? Why was he so unfortunate? Why had others new clothes, closets full, and he had not even one new garment? He could do nothing else but talk about the new coat which he would have some day.

Then he fell ill and was taken to the hospital. The cough grew worse. He was racked with pain. There he lay dreaming. In his dreams he saw new clothes and he heard the word "Tis-hadesh."

During the first days at the hospital the doctor came to see him daily. Now he came no more. Was it because he was getting better and would be out soon, to start life anew with the new coat? His strength ebbed little by little. His throat was parched, his tongue was dry, and his eyes burned with a strange fire.

Then his eyes closed gradually, and he beheld a wonderful vision. He saw angels descending, little angels, and big angels, thousands of angels, too many to count. The whole room was full of them. And the angels kept going up and down, up and down, fluttering their wings. Suddenly he saw that they all carried new white clothes for him in their outstretched arms. He heard a beautiful melody, and one word sung over and over again: "Tis-hadesh, Tis-hadesh."

Then a black angel appeared . . .

That day he was buried in new white clothes. But he did not hear "Tis-hadesh . . ."

The Factory

BY Abraham Reisin

It was winter. We boys were sitting in the heder studying. Suddenly the door opened and a cloud of steam filled the room. Berl the blacksmith, the father of one of the boys, closed the door and came in. He had come to find out how his son Yossel was getting along in school, and to exchange a few words with the teacher.

"*Shalom aleikhem,* Rabbi," said the blacksmith, as he extended his thick, toilworn hand.

"*Aleikhem shalom,*" my teacher answered, making an effort to smile. Since he smiled so seldom it was a thing which he found very difficult to do.

"Sit down, my friend," said the teacher. And, turning to us, "You rascals, study your lesson while I talk to Reb Berl."

We all buried our noses in our books, but our ears were straining to hear the news that Berl the blacksmith had brought.

"The things that go on today," the blacksmith began, shaking his head. "I tell you it's horrible, simply horrible."

"What do you mean, Reb Berl?" my teacher asked, lifting an eyebrow anxiously.

"Horrible, horrible," the blacksmith complained. "What a world, what a world."

"What is it?" the teacher asked encouragingly.

"Just horrible! Simply horrible!"

The other boys and I kept staring at our books and waited impatiently to find out what was so horrible.

"A little town," the blacksmith began. "Altogether only six streets and a market place. You see? And in such a town as ours they are going to build a factory. I tell you it's horrible."

"A factory," I said to the boy sitting next to me, kicking him in the leg.

"Study your lesson," the teacher said, and then he turned to the blacksmith. "Is that so? A factory here in town? They must be crazy!"

"A match factory."

"A match factory," I whispered to my friend and kicked him again.

"Are you studying or not!" the teacher shouted, grabbing my ear and giving it a good twist.

"Is that so, a match factory, here in town," the teacher mused as though he never had heard such astounding news. "How many matches does our town need? At the most two packages a week . . . Does it pay? It's crazy."

"Of course," the blacksmith calmly explained, "they're not puttng up a factory just to supply this town with matches. Matches, you understand, can be sold all over the world."

"In that case," the teacher frowned, "it makes sense. Who's putting up the factory?"

"Some rich fellow from Minsk. He's got a mint of money and is looking for business."

"And where is he building the factory?"

"He's got a wonderful spot for it, down by the brook."

"By the brook!" we cried out and looked at each other in bewilderment.

"Study, young ones! Back to your books!" the teacher shouted.

"By the brook," I said, and kicked my friend. My mind was full of strange visions of a factory right beside our old swimming hole.

After Passover the factory was finished. My friends and I

went down to look at it. The towering chimneys belched smoke angrily, as if they wanted to destroy the whole meadow.

"What high chimneys," Yoshke, one of my classmates, pointed out.

"Let's get closer. What are we afraid of?" said another encouragingly.

"Let's go," we all said. We stood by the brook. The water gurgled sadly. The little brook seemed to be crying. It seemed afraid of the huge factory.

We were gazing into the water when one boy remarked, "Look how dirty the water is now."

"That's right," another sighed, "It's from the chimney smoke."

"I feel sorry for the brook," said a boy, trying to make a joke.

"You're silly," we all said, and began to laugh. But the laughter was all on the outside; inwardly we were all heartsick and a little weepy.

After Shavuot the weather turned hot. One day we sat in school watching the shadows of the house across the street, hoping that they would grow longer. We wanted the sun to take pity on us and move rapidly behind the house, so that our teacher would let us out.

At last the whole street was in the shade. The village shepherd was herding his flock down the path when the teacher finally dismissed us.

"Let's go swimming," we shouted and ran down the street to the brook.

"Do you hear the whistle?" one of the boys panted as we hurried to the factory.

"Let it whistle, we don't care!" said another.

"That's right," we all agreed, whistling in the dark our-

selves.

But the closer we came to the brook, the more we felt that something was wrong.

And then suddenly we were there.

"The brook is gone!" I cried.

Whoo, whoo, whistled the chimneys.

Silently we examined what had once been our brook. The water looked like a plate full of cold left-over food scraps that had jelled. Its surface was covered with discarded wood, broken boxes, and garbage, and everything had a strange unpleasant odor.

We had been standing that way for several minutes, per-

Illustrated by E. Schloss

haps, when a coarse voice behind us rasped, "What are you doing here?"

We turned and saw a tall, pot-bellied, bald-headed man, with a broad smile on his face.

"What are you doing here?" he repeated.

"We came here to swim." one of the boys stammered out.

"Swim!" the fat man laughed. "Well, what are you waiting for? Ho, ho, ho!"

"We used to swim here once," another boy said with a break in his voice. "Once this water was clear."

"Sure, sure," said the pot-bellied man. "It was easy to swim here then. Let's see you do it now. That'd be quite a trick!" and he laughed again.

His laughter made us very angry, and one boy, pale as a sheet, cried, "I hope your factory burns down!"

"Ha, ha, ha," the fat man laughed. "Get out of here, you rascals!"

All the way home the man's laughter and the hum of the chimneys rang in my ears, and my heart was heavy with sorrow.

"I hope the factory burns down," one of the boys kept repeating.

"It choked our brook," said another.

And we mourned our brook a long time, and cursed the factory even longer.

It Is Good

BY ISAAC LOEB PERETZ

ON PASSOVER I am always reminded of the hassidic rabbi, the *Zayde* (grandfather) of Shpol.

In Russia, where I was born, many years ago, they had a law which permitted the police to seize a young boy from his home and parents and enroll him in the army for twenty-five years. Well, you can imagine that being among non-Jews in the army for a quarter of a century made it pretty difficult to remain a Jew, and since I was one of those young boys known as cantonists, who were kidnapped and enrolled in the army, I know what that means.

If I am a Jew today it is only because of the Zayde of Shpol. Of course, when I knew him before I was kidnapped, he was only a young man who had come to our town as a shohet. He used to come to our house to slaughter cattle and poultry and sometimes just to pass the time of day. I loved him. He had a wonderful way with children and could tell the most interesting stories.

After a while, for some reason or other, he decided to leave town. He came to our house to bid my father goodbye, and I cried and cried, and after he had left, I felt so bad that I followed him. I wanted to stay with him. Just how that could be managed, I did not know; nevertheless, I followed him. It was not easy for a small fellow like me to keep up with him. He walked briskly and soon he was lost from sight. I entered the woods, but since I could not see him, I sat under a tree to rest. Suddenly I heard a voice nearby. It sounded like his voice; I walked a little and soon caught sight of him. He was standing under a tree chanting *Shir Ha-Shirim,* the Song of Songs.

When he had done, he turned toward me and said, "Listen, Yudel" (that's my name) , "I have a request to make of you.

"I want you to remember your name, Yudel, for it comes from the Yiddish word that means 'Jew.' They are making you a cantonist. You will be going on a long journey. They will try to make you forget the Torah, your home and your parents. Probably they will succeed. But one thing I want you never to forget: Always remain a Jew."

With that he turned and swiftly vanished.

Two weeks later, they came for me and hustled me off to the army. I served far away from home, deep in the Russian wasteland, and never set eyes on a Jew.

As time passed, I often thought of making things easier by taking another name, but whenever such a thought came into my head, the rabbi appeared before me in my thoughts, saying: "Keep your name; remain a Jew!"

Once they flogged me and his image stood by me and seemed to wipe the cold sweat off my forehead; he stroked my face, and said softly, "Don't cry out! Suffer in silence! Remain a Jew!" I bore the punishment without a cry, without a moan.

Illustrated by Lazlo Matulay

Once I was standing sentry duty. It was evening and a bitter snowstorm was raging. I saw some people walking past me in the blinding snow, and one of them said in Yiddish, "This is the first night of Passover." The words fell on my heart like lead, and a longing came over me, a sort of heartache, that is impossible to describe. I wanted to recite the Haggadah, but I couldn't recall a word of it. Not even the Four Questions which I used to ask my father. I had known them when I was only six years old. If only I could have recalled a single word, the rest would have followed. But my mind was blank. I couldn't remember.

"Lord of the universe," I cried, "one word; help me with only one word!" Just then the phrase *"Avadim Hayinu—*we were slaves," came into my head. I was overjoyed. My prayer had been answered. And then the rest all came back to me, and as I paced up and down on my watch, with my musket on my shoulder, I recited and sang the Haggadah to the snowy world around. It poured out of me, word after word, like the links of a golden chain, like a string of pearls.

Meanwhile, the wind had died down. The snow had stopped falling, and the sky became clear. It was quiet and there was a peaceful, shimmering whiteness all around. Suddenly something bright and shining appeared. It was the figure of a man in a tallit. A silvery beard gleamed in the moonlight, and above the beard, two shining eyes and a wrinkled forehead. As it approached and passed me, it said, "It is good."

The words sounded like the strains of a violin. The figure vanished. But it was the eyes and the voice of the rabbi whom I had known when I was a child.

I went to Shpol when I was released from the Army. I went right to the Zayde of Shpol, and told him my story. And he did not seem at all surprised.

The Peddler

BY MAX ROBIN

YONAH was his name. His mother Leah was a shoemaker—
his mother, not his father. His father had died, and his wife
then took the place of her husband at the littered low
bench. Yonah was a little boy about whom everything was
long. His arms were spidery thin and long; so were his legs,
his ears and nose.

At first when he was too small to do anything more useful, he sat, a tiny living being, watching his mother at work.
His secret ambition then was to be a shoemaker himself. He
was deeply fond of mother Leah, whose pale face was set
off by clumps of black hair falling from under her kerchief,
which had once been white; and he longed for the day when
he would take her place at the manly art of shoe-repairing.

Yonah grew to a height when he could wear his father's
coat for an overcoat and tie the dried shoes with cord about
his feet. It was an event which marked the turning point in
his life. It was time to look around and do things. Do things
for his mother, to begin with. He had long been waiting for
this time.

He thought up a plan. It came to him all by itself, like an
inspiration. He would become the town's peddler! He
would sell—sell hot pancakes! It would be a novelty— a sen-
sation. People—storekeepers, flour-carriers, hawkers—who
spent the long day out in the cold, would be glad to buy.
How could they resist? His plan could not fail. He would
make money—more money than he would ever be able to
count.

The face of Leah darkened as she listened to her son's
plan. Look who would go out and earn his bread! Such a
little one. But he pleaded. And she gave her consent. They

136

went into business together — started a partnership — the mother doing the baking, the son the selling.

A little house, in a little town, the roof low, drooping with age and weariness. Winter. The darkness of dawn lightened by snow. Smoke trailing lazily in the frosty air, sharpening the stillness.

In front of an open oven a woman stands, like a shadow. The flame, drawn by the draft from the chimney, curls outward, and it brightens the face of the woman. A fresh odor of baking, familiar as the smell of fresh-mown hay, fills the dwelling. The woman bends and watches. Her face is peaceful in its reflected glow. On the wall the shadow of the flame in the oven is feebly panting for life.

The woman starts across the room.

"Yonah."

Out of the dimness, a vague stirring echoes back her call.

"Yonah!"

" Yes, Mamma! I am getting up!"

Cold in that end of the room. The window coated with a heavy lid of ice. But the darkness is fading. The flame has begun to dance on the wall.

And now the fire has died down in the oven. The shadow from its door has gone. A blue mist has begun to dissolve in the room. And two shadows, one bent, the other not yet, mysteriously glide about the room.

"Modeh ani l'fa'nekha . . ." murmurs a young voice in morning prayer.

The blue mist too has faded, revealing a boy standing wrapped in a long, long coat. The folds of his great trousers are tied at the ankles, tied with cord.

A lone, bleak figure **now** steps into the open. A basket hangs from his neck. Unmindful of the cold, he races toward the market.

The synagogues are lit. A door opens, there another closes; a man, all in an overcoat, steps out in the frost. His shoes crunch in the dry snow. Crunch-crunch-crunch, crunch-crunch . . . Gone is the man from the synagogue.

The market-place. An empty square. A flour-carrier, another, in their white, forever white garb, waiting to be hired, by the hour or the load. Upon this, upon him, a home depends, for its upkeep, its warmth . . . The first store has opened.

And now a new cry rises, rings through the air.

"Haiseh latkes! Pancakes!"

Yes, the day has begun . . .

Yonah peddled. He went out in the morning, returned home at noon. He then reappeared in the evening and stayed out late; strolled up and down the market place, his basket swinging, as he dashed this way and that.

"Hey. little one!" called a storekeeper who was too far from home to make more than one trip there a day.

Yonah obliged. His hand, out of the long sleeve, was in the basket.

"Pancakes?"

Boys were leaving their heders. They carried fancy paper lanterns, of different designs and colors. Their way did not always lead past the market place, but they were not going to miss the sight of the boy with the basket selling latkes.

They surrounded him, lanterns swinging, boys pushing one another to be close to the one in the center of the group.

"How do you sell your latkes?"

"A kopeck and two for a kopeck. Buy,buy! How many, how many?"

Some of the boys bought. The rest scattered, shouting and laughing as they ran, each one to his home, where perhaps a father and a mother were waiting.

Yonah remained.

"Haiseh latkes! Pancakes!"

He must sell all, all his wares. What could he do with any that might be left over?

If business was slow, or when he had grown weary of shouting his song, Yonah changed it; and he cried eagerly:

"Haiseh latkilach, haiseh . . ."

The chant was drawn-out and strange. A storekeeper heard it, and he poked his nose out in the cold. Yonah, the peddler-boy, the orphan . . .

Long after the boys from the heders had departed with their lanterns and the market place stood deserted and dark, a child's shrill voice still came crying through the frosty night.

"Heiseh latkes! Pancakes!"

There was despair in that cry. It sounded, at times, like a wail of pain and tears.

At last, though, Yonah too was going home, his basket

Illustrated by Isaac Friedlander

dangling before him. It was not yet empty; for wrapped in soft towels, a solitary fat latke, baked on a large dry leaf, had remained unsold. Must eat it now. But his hands were in his pockets as he munched and he counted. "Eighteen, eighteen and a half, nineteen—" The snow crunched, crunched under his feet . . .

The little house again. His home. He pushed the door and it pulled him in.

The inside was dark. Felt warm, too. Mother was sleeping.

Off went his basket. The latke-peddler moved carefully to his corner. Many cords to be untied. Knots that would not yield to numb fingers.

"Twenty kopecks, Mamma!" the boy cried happily to her across the room.

"Yonah," called Leah.

He was under covers, his long coat thrown over his shoulders. His toes were frozen. He doubled up. He had forgotten to recite the *Shema,* the bedtime prayer. He said it now, piously, seriously. And he was warm. He was happy. He shivered, but only out of happiness. Twenty kopecks—twenty kopecks . . .

"The Lord Is My Shepherd"

BY DAVID EINHORN

AT THE EDGE of a little town in Lithuania, long ago, stood an old house built of red bricks. The upper windows of colored glass formed a half circle. Four pillars supported the porch roof, and marble stairs veined with cracks led into the house. The area out front was overgrown with high grass sprouting wild amid sawed-off tree stumps. Tall and slender poplars had once grown here, but when the house had become a synagogue for the *Hevrah Tehillim*—the "Psalm-Reciters' Society"—they had been cut down. The walls, though, were covered on either side by spreading vines which reached up to the roof, where the swallows had built their nests.

The older people of the town held the Synagogue of the Psalm-Reciters in deep reverence and would tell the following strange story about it.

Many years before a very rich Jew, called Reb Shammai, had lived in the house. Reb Shammai was known everywhere, not so much for his riches or for his large business, but because he was a great scholar. And though it meant neglect of his business duties, he would shut himself up in a small room a few hours every day to study the Torah.

Reb Shammai had a servant called Yeruchem, a pious, honest Jew, though a simple one. No one thought of him as a scholar, but he knew the whole Book of Psalms by heart. He also was blessed with a fine voice, and no one could chant Psalms as beautifully as he.

Once a small group of ordinary Jewish laborers got together and established the Psalm-Reciters' Society, and they chose Yeruchem as their cantor.

Early every morning, when daylight had just begun to streak the sky with blue and the whole town was fast asleep, the Psalm-Reciters would gather in the old, large synagogue and their chanting voices would float over the roofs of the sleeping town.

When the rich scholar, Reb Shammai, reached his fiftieth year, he resolved to have a Sefer Torah written in gratitude to God for his wealth and wisdom. He ordered the necessary parchment and hired a famous old scribe, giving him the finest room in his house and supplying his family with all its needs. The scribe worked three years writing the Sefer Torah. When he had finished Reb Shammai made a great celebration for the whole town. The Sefer Torah was carried under a canopy by Reb Shammai himself into the synagogue. The musicians played in the street while all the townspeople marched in the procession. In the courtyard of the synagogue stood tables with honey cake and refreshments for everyone. There was a splendid feast prepared especially for the poor, and Shammai distributed fine gifts among them. At night he prepared a dinner in his house for all the scholars of the town and countryside.

The dinner was as grand as that of the weddings of the rich. The tables fairly groaned under the weight of the delicious food which the cooks and their assistants, whom Shammai had brought from the big city, had labored to prepare. Yeruchem was ordered by Shammai to see to it that the jugs of wine on the tables were kept full at all times.

In the middle of the meal Shammai suddenly noticed that the winejugs were empty, and that Yeruchem had disappeared. Shammai immediately sent a servant in search of Yeruchem. When the servant returned empty-handed, Shammai himself climbed to the small room in the attic of the house, where Yeruchem always went to recite the Psalms. He found him there, sitting on an old high-backed armchair, sunk in a deep sleep of exhaustion.

"Get up, you lazy Psalm-Reciter!" Shammai cried, poking Yeruchem rudely. "Come and serve the scholars!"

When Shammai came downstairs, he saw a man standing in the hall near the large door. He was dressed in the servants' livery of a neighboring nobleman with whom Shammai did business. The servant approached him and said, "Sir, the count awaits you outside in his carriage. He has an

important matter to discuss with you."

"I am very sorry," Shammai apologized, "but you can see that I have a house full of guests."

"It will not take long," the servant insisted.

Shammai yielded. He went out with the servant and saw the count's carriage hitched to four black horses in front of his house.

As he approached the carriage, its doors swung open and revealed to Shammai a man sitting inside, dressed in a large black traveling cloak and a hat whose brim covered his face.

"Sit down," the stranger said. And when Shammai sat down, the doors closed of themselves, and the four horses leaped from their places and began to race swiftly, as though carried by the wind, over fields and forests, mountains and valleys, rivers and lakes.

Shammai trembled with fear.

"Where are you taking me?" he asked.

"In a short while you will see."

Illustrated by E. Schloss

Suddenly a pine forest appeared in the distance. The forest grew nearer and larger, like a dense black wall. When it seemed they must crash into the trees, a road opened. The carriage drove into a wide courtyard and stopped before a great marble palace. All the windows were brightly lit. The stranger took Shammai's hand and led him into a large hall, which was flooded with such strong light that Shammai had to close his eyes for a moment. Seventy golden chairs were arranged in a half circle in the middle of the hall, and upon them sat dignified old men with white beards; opposite them, on a high golden throne, sat the Chief Justice.

The man who led Shammai in placed him on the defendant's chair and left the hall. At that moment a massive door opened, and a tall, handsome man wearing a golden crown and carrying a scepter in his hand appeared. Raising his voice, he turned to the seventy judges and said:

"Honored judges, Moses our teacher wrote down the Five Books of the Torah, in which we find the immortal commandments and laws which God gave His people Israel, to teach them how to lead good lives. I too wrote a book in five sections, the Book of Psalms. It contains prayers and songs to God, through which every poor man with a troubled spirit can pour out his heart to the Almighty. My Book of Psalms is part of the Bible, is it not? Why did this man Shammai, who stands before you so proudly because he had ordered a Sefer Torah to be written, shame and insult my servant Yeruchem, who has recited my Psalms all his life? Let Moses the son of Amram, come forward and testify!"

At that moment, an even larger door than the first one opened, and there appeared an old man whose face shone like the sun, holding God's staff in his hand. And now David, King of Israel, and Moses, Prophet and Lawgiver, faced each other!

Suddenly, everything vanished from Shammai's sight, and he found himself before the door of his house.

Shammai went back into the hall where the guests were waiting for him. He sat down in his seat and placed Yeruchem next to himself and gave him much honor.

Early next morning, when the first glimmer of day touched the eastern horizon and the whole town was still asleep, one could see Reb Shammai walking with his servant Yeruchem, the Psalm-Reciter, to the old synagogue to recite Psalms.

Shammai lived for many years, and when he knew his days were numbered, he donated his beautiful house to the Psalm-Reciters' Society, so that it might have its own synagogue.

Translated from the Yiddish by Morris Epstein

Tevye Finds a Son-in-Law

BY SHOLOM ALEICHEM

MODERN children, did you say? Ah, you slave for them day and night—and what do you get out of it?

To make a long story short, I had just lost everything I had in a stock market investment, and I was very low. It looked as if it was all over with me.

"Fool," my wife says to me. "You'll get nowhere worrying. Go out for a while. Go see Lazer-Wolf, the butcher. He wants to see you about something very important."

"What is he so anxious to see me about? If he wants to buy that cow of ours, let him knock the idea out of his head."

"Tevye, enough of that!" she comes back at me. "You go over and see Lazer-Wolf. Every Thursday when our daughter Tzeitel goes there for meat, he says, 'You tell your father to come and see me. It's important.' "

So I let her talk me into it, and I go over to see Lazer-Wolf.

"Well, Reb Tevye," he says, "let's have some tea and talk business. I tried to reach you through your daughter. You understand, I've been casting an eye . . ."

"I know," I say, "but it's no use."

"Why not?" he asks. "It seems to me that you have a few more without her."

"Does it bother you if I keep them?" I say. "If anyone is jealous of my milk-cow . . ."

Lazer-Wolf throws back his head and lets out a roar. "That's a good one!" he howls at me. "A cow! I'm talking about your daughter Tzeitel! I want to marry her. Let's shake hands on it and call it a match."

Well, I couldn't say a word. All I could think was: Lazer-Wolf . . . Tzeitel . . . He had children as old as she was. But then I reminded myself: what a lucky thing for her. She'll have everything she wants. And if he is not so good-looking? There were other things besides looks!

"Well, Reb Tevye," he says. "**Why** don't you say something?"

"I won't stand in your way," I replied. "But there's Tzeitel herself to be asked."

"What foolishiness!" says Lazer-Wolf. "Is this something to *ask* her about? *Tell* her, Reb Tevye! Go home, tell her what is what, and get the wedding canopy ready. But first, Reb Tevye, let's have a little drink. How about it?"

Well, we took a drop or two—and when I came home it was late at night and my wife, seeing right away that I was tipsy, gave me a proper welcome.

"Sh . . . Golde, control yourself. Congratulations, Golde,"

I say to her. "Our Tzeitel is engaged to be married."

And I tell her the whole story from start to finish, how and what and when and why. And is she happy!

Next day I got through my work as fast as I could. I got back into my cart and started for home again, joyous as could be.

Suddenly, when I'm getting close to home, I see someone coming toward me. It's Tzeitel. She falls on my neck with a sob.

"What are you crying for?" I ask. "If you say *no* its *no*. May God send you a husband worthy of you, and may he come soon, Amen."

Well, we came home at last. I sat down on the grass near the house to think up some fantastic tale to tell my wife.

And then I heard someone call out, "Good evening, Reb Tevye." I looked up and saw a familiar face—Motel, a young tailor from Anatevka. "I have been wanting to come here for a long time, Reb Tevye," he says at last, "only all of us tailors have as much as we can do right now. It's been a summer of weddings. Everybody is marrying off his children."

"Everybody," I say. "Everybody except Tevye."

"It all depends on you, Reb Tevye."

"So?" I ask. "Maybe you have a match for Tzeitel?"

"A perfect fit!" the tailor answers.

"And who, may I ask, is the man? Tell me!"

"Who is it?" he says. "Why, me—myself!"

When he said that I jumped up from the ground as if I'd been scalded, but he goes right on talking. "Here is the whole story," he says. "Your daughter Tzeitel and I gave each other our pledge more than a year ago now that we would marry . . ."

"And where do I come in?" I ask him bluntly. "Doesn't

anyone have to ask a father any more?"

"On the contrary," says Motel, "that's exactly why I came to talk to you."

To make a long story short he talked me into it. But what was I going to do about my Golde? I go to bed. But I can't sleep. At last I come upon the right plan. Listen, I'll tell you . . .

It's past midnight. Suddenly I let out a horrible yell: "Help! Help! Help!" Everybody wakes up, and first of all —Golde. "Wake up, Tevye!" she gasps, and shakes me.

I open my eyes and call out in terror. "Where is she? Where is she?"

"Where is who?" asks Golde. "What are you talking about?"

I can hardly answer. "The ghost of Fruma-Sarah, Lazer-Wolf's first wife . . . She was standing here a minute ago. Oh, it's lucky you woke me up or I'd have died of fright right on the spot. Oh, what a dream! We were having a celebration of some kind, when in comes your grandmother Tzeitel, may her soul rest in peace . . ."

Illustrated by Bill Giacalone

"Grandmother Tzeitel!" my wife shouts, turning pale as a sheet. "How did she look? How was she dressed?"

"May our enemies look the way she looked. 'Congratulations,' she said, 'I am so happy that you picked such a fine young man for your Tzeitel who bears my name. He's a fine, upstanding lad—this Motel . . . and even if he is a tailor he's still an honest boy . . .' "

"A tailor!" gasps Golde.

"Don't interrupt me," I tell her. "When I heard her congratulate me, I said to her, 'You mean a butcher, don't you? A butcher named Lazer-Wolf?'

" 'No,' says your grandmother again. 'No, Tevye. Your daughter is engaged to Motel, and he's a tailor, and she'll grow old with him in comfort and honor.'

"I looked up, and there is Fruma-Sarah—Lazer-Wolf's first wife—and this is what she says: 'Reb Tevye, why should you do a thing like this—let your daughter take my place, live in my house, carry my keys, wear my clothes, my jewelry, my pearls?'

"And with these words Fruma-Sarah grabs me by the windpipe and begins choking me!"

"Oh," cries Golde. "If my grandmother—may she rest in peace—took the trouble to come all the way from the other world to congratulate us, why, all we can do is say that this is all for the best, and it couldn't possibly be any better. Amen. Selah . . ."

Well, why should I go on and on?

The next day they were engaged, and not long after were married. And the two of them, praise the Lord, are happy. He does his own tailoring, and she is busy day and night, cooking and baking and washing and tidying and bringing water from the well . . . They barely make enough for food. But if you ask her—my Tzeitel, I mean—she says everything is as good as it could be. Just let Motel stay in good health.

So go complain about modern children. You slave for them, do everything for them! And they tell you that they know better.

And . . . maybe they do . . .

The Hoshana of Rabbi Ephraim

BY DAVID EINHORN

THE ENDLESS Russian plains stretch as far as the eye can see. Here and there a lake dots the landscape, with lush, green grass fringing the water's edge. In olden times, scattered villages nestled in the hills and dales bordering the lakes.

Once, a Jewish village lay sprawling near just such a lake. To get to the water, one walked a short distance from the town, climbed a sloping hill, and there it was—its surface like a gleaming mirror reflecting the deep blue of heaven. The horizon was unbroken save for one old willow tree whose drooping branches swayed in eternal mourning. Occasional drops of water fell from the branches like tears and made rippling circles in the still water. To the Jews of the village the tree became known as "Ephraim's Hoshana."

Many years ago (said the old folks) a wealthy man lived in the village. He had an only child, a brilliant boy named Ephraim.

His schoolmates called him "the curious dreamer" because he asked so many questions and because he spent whole summer days at the lake, lost in daydreams.

Each Sukkot his father would assign a task to Ephraim, a duty which the boy considered a great honor.

In those days of primitive transportation, an etrog and

lulav were very expensive. They had to be brought from far overseas, and only the wealthiest people could afford them. Those who were fortunate enough to own an etrog and lulav considered it a mitzvah to lend them to the poor so that they might pronounce the blessing.

Every morning, Ephraim made his rounds with the etrog and lulav. First he went to the old yeshiva teacher, Rabbi Isaiah, who lived with his wife in a little village. Rabbi Isaiah was too feeble to get about much, and he could always be found poring over a holy book.

Rabbi Isaiah and Ephraim had become fast friends. The old man was the only one to whom the boy could confide his innermost thoughts.

"Your son will one day be a great rabbi," the teacher often said to Ephraim's father.

Once, when Ephraim brought the etrog and lulav to Rabbi Isaiah, the old man's attention was drawn to the lad's troubled expression. "What is it, my boy?" said the rabbi.

"Nothing," said Ephraim. "But . . . I just cannot understand the meaning of the etrog and the lulav, the myrtle and the willow branches."

"My child," answered the rabbi, "you know the explanations our sages have given us."

"I know," said Ephraim, "but I'm still puzzled."

"Well then," said the rabbi with a smile, "perhaps you will like my explanation. The lulav is a palm leaf. A palm tree reaches skyward and its leaves are like hands outstretched to heaven in prayer. The etrog has a delicate fragrance, and good deeds, say our sages, have the aroma of rare spices.

"The myrtle twigs, my child, represent beauty and modesty. The Hebrew word for myrtle is *hadassah* and that, as you know, was Queen Esther's name, for she was very beautiful. But it is also said that when Adam was driven from

the Garden of Eden because he ate from the tree of knowledge, he took with him a myrtle branch. Later he planted it. It flowered beautifully, and when Adam looked at it, he dreamed that one day the whole world would be a Garden of Eden. We, too, wait and hope for the Messiah."

"And what about the willow branch . . . . the hoshana?" asked Ephraim. "Why do we mistreat it so? At the morning service on Hoshana Rabbah, we beat the poor willow against the floor until all its leaves are gone! And didn't our ancestors hang their harps on the willows of Babylon because they were in exile? The willow has followed us everywhere."

"Yes, my child," said the rabbi. "It is a sign of our sadness and our longing. When we dream of being freed from exile, we thrash the symbol of our exile."

"I like the poor willow best of all. It is sad and lonely . . . like me." Ephraim's voice broke.

Rabbi Isaiah leaned over and said softly, "Bring three hoshanot—three willow branches—tomorrow. I will bless two

Illustrated by E. Schloss

with the etrog and lulav. The third I will bless separately
and you will plant it near your favorite spot at the lake.
Then we shall see what happens."

Ephraim did as he was bidden.

Years passed. Ephraim became a renowned rabbi. Isaiah
died. And the little twig that the boy had planted blossom-
ed into a great willow with massive branches and thick
leaves. Rabbi Ephraim forgot all about his talk with Rabbi
Isaiah. Nor did he know how the old teacher had blessed
the third hoshana.

Then one day Emperor Napoleon marched into Russia
with his armies. Soldiers in strange uniforms appeared.
They blocked the roads and ordered the inhabitants of the
little village to stay indoors.

Now it happened that Ephraim had gone to a wedding
in a town an hour away from his home. He had decided to
return on foot. Dusk had fallen when he reached the outskirts of his village. Suddenly he heard a sharp command,
and he was startled to see armed men, shouting orders in
a language he did not understand, pointing rifles threaten-
ingly at him.

Panic seized Ephraim and he began to run. With the
soldiers at his heels he came to the little vale. A mysterious
force seemed to spin him around, and against his will he
panted up the sloping hill and down toward the lake.

Then something beyond belief happened. The dense foli-
age of the old willow tree parted and enfolded Ephraim like
two protecting arms. Dumbfounded, he saw the branches
weave themselves into a sheltering screen. When the French
soldiers came charging up to the lake they found no trace
of a human being. The company commander snarled, "He
couldn't have gotten through here. He'd need an axe to
chop open a path. Probably ran to the village." And they

left.

For two days and nights Ephraim remained in his hide-away. The long green willow leaves splashed raindrops into Ephraim's cupped palms, and he was refreshed. On the second day, sitting in silence in his shady shelter, Ephraim suddenly remembered his talk with Rabbi Isaiah. A tremor passed through him. This tree was the third hoshana which Isaiah had blessed and which Ephraim had planted!

No sooner had he remembered than the branches parted again. Ephraim saw the open path and knew that it was safe to return home.

To be sure, the French soldiers had departed. The villagers greeted Rabbi Ephraim joyfully. They had been certain that misfortune had befallen him.

The very next Sabbath, Ephraim came to the synagogue and recited *Gomel,* the blessing recited by those who are rescued from danger. In his sermon he recounted his talk of long ago with Rabbi Isaiah and described how he had planted the third hoshana which had so miraculously saved him from Napoleon's troops.

And he took a vow in the presence of the whole congregation. "Some day, God willing," he said, "I will journey to the Holy Land with my family. When I go, I will take with me a shoot of this willow and plant it near Jerusalem, so that the willow will be blessed to see the arrival of the Messiah."

"Who knows," he concluded, his voice trailing into a whisper, "perhaps branches of this very willow may one day grace the holy altar of our rebuilt Temple of God."

Translated from the Yiddish by Morris Epstein

Purim Player

EVERYONE knew Simon the Redhead. Simon was an orphan. At the age of eight he had to look out for himself. To earn his living he did jobs. He worked at the bakery, helped the glazier with the window panes, stretched skins in the tannery, watered the coachman's horses. He was busy all year round.

But there was one day of the year when Simon the Redhead forgot about all his chores and enjoyed a holiday. That day was Purim.

On Purim he was just like the other boys on the street. All the children wore masks and no one recognized the other. With masked faces, all were alike—the rich and the poor. You couldn't tell the difference between Simon the Redhead and Berel the miller's son. You would not even know which was Meyer, the only son of the rich manufacturer who lived in the village.

However, the truth is that even on Purim, Simon had a complaint.

The boys who dressed as Purim players always insisted that Simon play the part of Haman. At first, Simon readily played the role of the villain. But after a few years he rebelled.

"I want to play Mordecai once," he said.

"Listen to him!" the others jeered. "He thinks we'll let *him* play Mordecai. If you don't want the part, we'll get another Haman."

Simon's face was beet-red. Trembling with anger, he cried out:

"I'm Haman every year. Why doesn't Meyer or David or somebody else play the part? It's Purim, isn't it? It's just

make believe!"

Nothing helped. The boys were angry. They found another Haman and Simon was left out of the play.

That Purim Simon was alone. But his mind was made up. He would show them! He would dress as Mordecai, go from house to house, sing a Purim song, make a Purim speech, and act the part so well that everyone would recognize him as Mordecai the Righteous.

But he needed a beard, a long robe, a sash. He had none of these things, and soon the day was almost over. Families were already sitting down to their Purim feast, all dressed in holiday finery. The Purim players were gathering in

Illustrated by Gabe Josephson

groups, wearing costumes and masks, some in their parents' old clothes.

Desperately, Simon ran to Reuben the baker, who smeared his chin, his lips and cheeks with soot and ashes from the oven. He turned his hat and tattered coat round, back to front, and ran out into the street ready to play Mordecai.

Unasked and uninvited, he came into homes all by himself—a Mordecai without a Haman, without a king, even without a royal guard. But wherever he went, he acted his part bravely, and people applauded and filled his pockets with jingling coins.

The boys on the street soon learned about Simon's success. The very next day, they promised him that next Purim they would gladly let him play Mordecai.

That night Simon slept a sweet sleep. He had been a real hero for once in his life.

Too Late

BY ABRAHAM REISIN

ANTOSH cracked his whip, and urged his ancient mare along. It was almost noon and he was only on the outskirts of the town. But the poor old horse just plodded along. Antosh lifted his whip again. "Please move!" The horse whinnied, and it seemed that even *she,* was laughing at Antosh. But what could he expect? Everyone else whom he had passed on the road had laughed. Everyone . . . What could be wrong?

It had all begun when autumn came.

The days in eastern Europe were getting shorter and the nights longer. Antosh, a peasant living in a small village, would have liked to light a lamp in the evening, but the kerosene jug was empty and he had no money. His supply of salt was also running very low, and he only had a very small piece of soap left. There was not a tea leaf in the pot, nor a pinch of snuff in the jar.

"It's bad," said Antosh, talking to himself, "no salt, no tobacco, no soap, nothing."

And Antosh had no way of earning money. He had only one hope: to load his wagon with the green branches that the Jews use to cover their sukkahs, take it into town and sell it.

Right after Rosh Hashanah, he began to pester the one Jew who lived in his village.

"When will you celebrate Sukkot?" he used to ask every day.

And each time the Jew would answer, "It's a long way off yet."

"But when?" Antosh would insist.

One day, the Jew, to stop Antosh's pestering, answered, "One week from today."

Actually it was only five days to Sukkot, but Antosh did not know this, and planned to come to town with his merchandise when he thought it was two days before the holiday. This was, of course, the first day of Sukkot.

That day Antosh rose early, hitched up his sleepy, half-starved horse, took his axe and drove into the forest. He began to cut branches and put them into the wagon. He chose the longer and thicker branches. "Good merchandise sells better," he thought. The load continued to grow and at last the wagon was full.

Now Antosh drove slowly, and as he drove he was thinking of the soap, tobacco, flour, and other things he would be able to buy with the money he earned from the sale of his merchandise.

When he reached the outskirts of the town and saw that the sukkahs were all covered, his heart skipped a beat and his head began to whirl. He steadied himself and thought. "It is the same every year. Some Jews cover their sukkahs early and others later."

He rode on. Two women were standing in front of a house. They were pointing at him and laughing.

"Why are you laughing?" Antosh asked angrily.

"Because you brought the branches so early," they mocked.

"What do you mean, early?" Antosh asked, not understanding why they made fun of him. He was answered by peals of laughter. Antosh spat angrily and rode on thinking to himself, "How can it be? If I counted right today is two days before the holiday."

He broke out in a cold sweat, because it occurred to him that he might have lost count of the days. He was too late. Certainly, too late. All the sukkahs were covered. He would have no salt, no tobacco.

Sadly he drove on and his horse, who seemed to sense her master's misfortune, pulled the wagon with head bowed.

At last he reached the village square. "I have green twigs and branches for your sukkah," he called. "Who will buy roof-coverings from Antosh?"

His voice echoed back. Except for a goat or two ambling along the road, the square was deserted. And then, suddenly, the big doors of the synagogue in the center of the square swung open and the men started pouring out. Jews in well-brushed black coats and fur-trimmed hats, little boys whose sidecurls had barely begun to grow. And they all seemed to be heading toward Antosh.

Ah, here they were! Now he could sell his wares. He cried,

"Here is Antosh the woodchopper with twigs for your suk-kahs. I have branches, I have . . ." Antosh stopped.

The crowd had surrounded Antosh and his w a g o n. "Thank you for coming," said one. "Only—you are a little late. One little day late. Can't you see that it is already Suk-kot? That today is the holiday itself?"

"Everyone's sukkah is already covered," said another.

But Antosh, confused by his misfortune, cried, "Buy, buy, I need salt, I need tobacco, I need soap . . ."

The crowd around the peasant stopped laughing. Even Antosh grew silent. He lowered his head in misery and shame. No use standing there like the big oaf he was. Might as well go home and eat his twigs. The people looked at the poor, hungry peasant, saw his worried face, and felt sorry for him.

"A poor peasant; it's a pity," one of them said.

"He had high hopes, and all of a sudden, nothing," said another.

"We ought to buy his green branches," another man

Illustrated by Isaac Friedlander

suggested.

"But how can we? It's holiday today," his neighbor asked.

"No salt, no kerosene, no soap," the peasant continued to cry.

"Wait a minute," said someone. "Listen to me, everybody." The speaker jostled his way through the crowd. Clambering up on Antosh's wagon, he shouted to the townsfolk:

"Antosh has worked so hard. He meant well. It's our duty to help him now. And we *can* help him. We don't have to *pay* him. He doesn't need money. He needs merchandise—food and kerosene. We can't let him go away empty-handed. Won't you open your shops and give Antosh what he needs in return for his labors?"

Everyone was quiet for a moment. Then Jonah the baker said in his deep voice, "He is right. I will give Antosh six loaves of bread." And Reuben the grocer nodded, "I'll throw in five cans of kerosene." And David the fishdealer said, "I give two pickerel and seven carp."

Then they all chimed in and offered tobacco and barley and rice until Antosh's wagon was filled with all kinds of good things.

Antosh had never known such kindness in all his life. The peasant was beside himself with joy. He did not know whether to laugh or cry. Slowly he stood up in his wagon.

"Dear people," he stammered, "Antosh cannot make speeches. He can only say he is grateful. He says it now. Antosh is grateful."

He sat down.

As he was about to drive away, someone gave him a big piece of hallah.

"Here, take it home," he was told.

"Here's another piece," said someone else. Then everyone began to bring Antosh hallah. He was so confused that he could only murmur over and over, "Thank you. Thank you!"

Everyone was happy. Mordecai, a jolly Jew who spared nothing in celebrating the holidays, and who had a future son-in-law visiting him, brought out a glass of whiskey for Antosh. "Here, drink this and farewell," he said.

Antosh swallowed the whiskey in one gulp, took a bite of hallah, and cried out, "I'll never forget it, never!"

The Unexpected Guest

BY MOSHE DLUZNOWSKY

THE RIVER rose a few days before Passover. The snow, piled in heavy drifts on the mountains, had begun to melt under the warm rays of the early spring sun. The trickling drops swelled into gushing torrents roaring down the mountain-side. The rivers bellied, overfilled, and flooded roads and bypaths, silent fields and muddy streets.

Dov Ber and his wife Hannah lived in a little house near a river. From the window, they could see the lumber rolling. Logs, thousands of them, floating downriver, tied into rafts, driven by loggers. The river was black with logs.

Dov Ber, the blacksmith, and Hannah lived alone. Their children had left for the big city many years ago. They did not want to live in the small village by the river, so they had left home to seek their fortune. The smith and his wife were content and happy that the Almighty had given them health, good years, food to eat, a pillow to rest their heads on.

They were quiet, God-fearing people. A poor man never

left their house hungry, and weary travelers could interrupt their journey and stay with Dov Ber for as long as they pleased.

Now it was but one day to Passover, Hannah had cleaned the house, scoured the pots and pans, shined the silver cups and wine glasses, and made all the necessary preparations to greet the Passover holiday with great joy.

Dov Ber stood at the window. The river seemed angry and vicious as it lapped against its banks, threatening to encircle the house and set it awash. A lashing rain pounded on the window panes. Logs and rafts strained against their ropes, tore apart, splintered and crashed as the waters tossed them about like match-sticks.

But Dov Ber's thoughts were only on the festival. "How will we find a guest for Passover?" he murmured to himself. "No human being will be out traveling in this weather. Who will ask the Four Questions at my Seder this Pesah?"

"Never was there such a flood," Hannah sighed. "We will have to sit at the Seder alone. Still, Dov Ber, when you go to the Bet Ha-Midrash for evening services, perhaps you will find a poor Jew who will want to sit at our table."

"The river may swallow our house. In this weather, will there be a stranger at the synagogue?" Dov Ber said with sorrow in his voice.

Nevertheless, Dov Ber searched for a stranger at services. But only familiar faces met his glance. He went home with a heavy heart. The raindrops pelted his face, but he did not bow his head. His feet sloshed through water and mud, but he paid no attention. He entered his house, said *"Gut Yom-Tov"* to Hannah, and prepared to conduct the Seder alone, just he and his wife, and he would ask the Four Questions himself.

The table was set beautifully. The silver and the glass

goblets shone. The flames of the candles in the silver candle-sticks danced. The red wine in the crystal bottle merrily reflected the candlelight.

Outside the wind moaned and whined as if goblins were celebrating a wedding. The river was rising, still rising, as if to engulf the world.

Dov Ber put on a kittel, the white linen robe that he always wore at the Seder. Hannah wore a black silk dress and around her throat a strand of pearls. They tried to forget their deep longing for a guest at the Seder table. After all, it was a holiday, and one must not be sad.

Illustrated by Ben Einhorn

Hannah started to fill the glasses with wine. Dov Ber opened the Haggadah. Suddenly, with rending force, the stormy wind broke open the door and swept through the house, echoing against the walls like peals of thunder. Above the wind came a desperate scream, a choking cry for help.

The couple paled. Hannah's hands trembled and her glass of wine fell and shivered to pieces on the floor. Dov Ber shuddered and pulled himself together.

"Someone is in trouble!" he said, rising from the table.

In a very short while he came back, dragging a man who was drenched from head to toe, who was so waterlogged that he could hardly stand on his feet.

The stranger lifted his eyes, looked about and said weakly:

"A Jewish home! God be praised."

"God has sent us a guest for the Seder," Dov said happily.

They took off the stranger's wet clothing, bundled him up in warm dry things, and made him comfortable.

The man's name was Daniel. He was a logger, he said, and had been rolling lumber from an inland forest to the port of Danzig. He had started out on the river a few days ago, intending to arrive in the big city of Danzig in time for the Passover holiday. On the second day, a stormy wind had torn apart the rafts. Daniel had clung desperately to a log, the wind and the waves battering him back and forth along the river, and finally tossing him out of the river almost onto Dov Ber's doorsteps.

Daniel the logger sat at the Seder and asked the Four Questions. The house of Dov Ber the blacksmith and his wife Hannah was filled with holiday joy and happines, because God had sent them a guest. They were able to fulfill the mitzvah of having a Seder, with a guest at the table.

The Great Ink Flood

BY SHOLOM ALEICHEM

"ONE HUNDRED rubles a month and over can be earned by anyone who acquaints himself with the contents of our book which costs only one ruble plus postage."

As soon as my brother Eli read this advertisement in a newspaper, he sent the ruble—his very last ruble—and told Mother she need not worry any longer.

At last, the book arrived. Goodness! So many ways to make money. A formula for making ink. A formula for shoe polish. A formula for exterminating mice, cockroaches, and other nasty things.

Ink, said Eli, is a good business. He went to ask Yudel the

Illustrated by Gabe Josephson

writing teacher how much he spent on ink. Yudel said, a fortune! Eli decided to try ink.

My brother Eli bought a sack of powder and a huge bottle of glycerine. He mixed the ingredients in a large pot, put it into the oven. Then we carefully poured the mixture into our cider barrel. Then we filled the barrel halfway with water, and my brother Eli said, "Enough!" He ordered us to bring him a new pen and white paper. He dipped the pen into the barrel and started to make zigzags on the paper. He showed the writing first to Mother, then to his wife, Brocha. They both took a look and said, "It writes!"

We poured in several more buckets of water, until the b a r r e l was full. Then my brother raised his hand, "Enough!" and all of us sat down to eat.

After the meal, we started to pour the ink into bottles. All sorts—big and small. Beer bottles, wine bottles, cider bottles, brandy bottles and—just bottles.

The work went well and gaily. The only trouble was that the ink messed up our fingers, hands, noses, faces . . . my brother and I became as black as prunes.

I can't tell you how much ink we had. I guess there were a thousand bottles. But what of it, when there was no place to put them? My brother Eli went everywhere. "There's no sense in selling retail," my brother announced. "I'll sell wholesale!"

And Eli went to make the rounds of the shops. He came to a large dealer with a sample, but the dealer wouldn't touch it because it had no label. He said the bottle must have a label with a picture. My brother Eli said, "I don't make pictures—I make ink!" The dealer retorted, "Well, go ahead and make it!"

My brother went to Yudel the writing teacher, but Yudel gave him a real shock. It seems he had already provided himself with enough ink for the entire summer. My brother asked, "How many bottles did you buy?" Said Yudel, "Bottles? I bought one single bottle of ink. When it's used up I'll buy another one . . ."

My brother Eli didn't know what to do with all the ink. He said he would start selling retail.

My brother Eli bought a large square of paper. He sat down and printed with big letters:

INK FOR SALE
WHOLESALE & RETAIL
NICE AND CHEAP

Many people passed our door and stopped to look. I saw them through the window. My brother said, "Go out, stand at the door, and listen to what they're saying."

I stood there for half an hour and then returned. My brother Eli asked me softly, "Well, what did they say?"

"They said it's printed very nicely."

"Is that all?"

"That's all."

Mother set the table. We washed and sat down to eat. We were very crowded for space. The bottles left no room in the house. We barely managed to sit down, when in flew a spry youngster. I knew him. His name was Koppel, and his father was a ladies' tailor.

"Do you sell ink retail here? I'd like to buy some."

"How much?"

"Give me a penny's worth."

My brother was ready to explode. But he controlled himself and poured him a penny's worth of ink. Hardly a quarter of an hour passed when in walked a girl. I didn't know her. She picked her nose and addressed Mother:

"You make ink here?"

"Certainly!"

"Sister would like to know if you could lend her some ink. She has to write a letter to her sweetheart in America."

"Who is your sister?"

"Basia, the seamstress."

"Is that so! Just see how she's grown! I didn't even recognize her! Have you got an inkwell with you?"

"What would we be doing with an inkwell? My sister also wants to know if you could lend her a pen to write the letter with, and she'll return the ink and the pen to you . . ."

My brother Eli left the table. He was in the other room. He was walking around silently, looking down at the ground and biting his fingernails.

A week later, my brother Eli walked up and down the room racking his brains. What was to be done with all the ink?

"Ink again?" asked Mother.

"I'm no longer thinking about the ink," said my brother Eli. "I'm thinking about the bottles. There's a fortune in those bottles. They've got to be emptied so that we can

make some money on them."

But where could one pour out so much ink? That was a problem.

"There's nothing to be done about it," said Eli. "We must wait until evening. It's dark in the evening, and nobody will see us."

Then we carried out bottle after bottle and emptied them all out. Soon a river was formed. "We mustn't pour in one place," said my brother, and I obediently poured in a different place every time. Every bottle into another spot. There was the neighbor's wall—swish! The neighbor's fence—swish! Two goats gazing at the moon and chewing their cud—swish!

Early next morning our neighbors rose and raised a shout. "Murder!" Somebody's wall was all spotted with ink. Another's fence was all messed up—a brand new fence! A third one used to have two white goats. Now they were black and we couldn't recognize them . . .

As soon as it grew dark we filled our pockets with bottles and took them to the river. We poured all the ink out, brought the empty bottles home and carried back a fresh load. We worked all night long.

Our ink made the river a little larger. We must have poured at least a thousand bottles into it. We worked like slaves. We fell asleep like dead, and were awakened by Mother's wail:

"Unhappy woman that I am! What did you do to the river?"

It seems that we ruined the whole town. The washer-women had nowhere to wash clothes. The coachmen could not water their horses. The water-carriers wanted to come and have it out with us . . .

But we decided not to wait for the water-carriers. My

brother Eli and I put our best feet forward and marched off to our friend Pinney.

"They can look for us there," said my brother Eli, taking me by the hand, and we disappeared to our friend Pinney.

How Eliezer Was Tested

BY DAVID EINHORN

NOT FAR from a town, amidst towering mountains and near a river, stood a lonely inn owned by a man called Eliezer and his wife Hannah.

Not many people stopped at the inn. From time to time riverboats would draw up to the inn and buy spices, or a wayfarer passing through the pine-covered mountains would rest there.

Eliezer and Hannah received all guests, rich and poor alike, with a warm welcome. And when a poor traveler came to the inn, they received him with open arms and gave him a good meal, a clean bed, and even a little money.

Though Eliezer and Hannah had no children, they felt no bitterness towards God. They did as many good deeds as they could. Once, Eliezer and Hannah's names were spoken of in heaven, where it was said that there were no such God-fearing, kindly people on earth as they; that their home was open to all poor travelers, just as our Father Abraham's was.

But Satan, who was standing by, said, "You can trust no human being until you have tested him. Send me to Eliezer, and we shall test him."

When Elijah the Prophet heard these words, he feared that Satan might harm Eliezer. Elijah said, "Send *me* instead, and I will test him."

It was decided in heaven to send Elijah.

One Friday evening, the house of Eliezer was already prepared for the Sabbath. The table was laid with a snow-white cloth, the two *challot* were covered by a small colored cloth, and the candles in the four silver candlesticks were ready to be lit by Hannah.

Suddenly the door opened, and in walked a man dressed in rags and wearing torn, dirty shoes. His small blue eyes were dull as a drunkard's, and his nose was fiery red. He approached the Sabbath table and shouted drunkenly, "Give me something to drink!"

Hannah went to the kitchen and brought out a bowl of noodle soup and some meat. The stranger neither washed his hands nor made a blessing over the food, but began eating immediately. When he had finished, he said, "Give me something to drink!"

"Tea, perhaps?" asked Hannah.

"No, whiskey . . . a whole bottle."

After he had gulped down the whiskey, he arose.

"I want to go to sleep."

Eliezer led him to a clean bed. The drunkard sank down in his muddy clothing and filthy shoes.

The same thing happened the next day. As soon as the man woke up, he demanded whiskey and f o o d . Then, stretching out on a bench, he insulted Eliezer and Hannah in coarse and rude language.

At night, after Eliezer had recited *havdalah* to mark the end of the Sabbath, the drunkard pulled himself together and prepared to leave.

Eliezer politely walked with him to the door, and placed a small sum of money in his hand.

At that very moment, the drunkard disappeared, and Eliezer saw in the moonlight an old and dignified man with a white beard. The old man grasped Eliezer by the hand, and said:

"I am the Prophet Elijah, sent from heaven to test you. Now, tell me what it is you wish, and it shall be done."

"A son," Eliezer answered.

"For this you will have to undergo another test," said Elijah. "Have courage and your wish will be fulfilled."

A short time later, Eliezer sat at the window of his inn watching the sun set behind the mountains. The peaks glowed red, and the last rays of the sun were reflected from the tips of the pine trees and the purple fog bank hovering over the river. As Eliezer thought about the mysteries of God's world, he suddenly saw a ship cutting through the low-hanging fog. It dropped anchor close to Eliezer's inn. Several men scrambled ashore, and before Eliezer could cry out they had tied his arms and carried him to the vessel and away to sea.

After several days, the ship came to a large seaport. Eliezer was dragged to the slave market and sold to a minister of the king.

He worked very hard and his record of good service came to the attention of the minister, who appointed Eliezer his personal servant.

Once, when his master came home and Eliezer went to greet him with a basin of warm water and a towel, as was

his custom, he saw that something was wrong.

"Why does my lord look so sad?" Eliezer asked. "Perhaps I can help you."

"Ah, my dear Eliezer," said the master, "near our land lives a wicked people. Now they have gathered a great army and are marching against us. Our king has ordered me to find a way to save our land."

That night Eliezer had a dream. He was told all that must be done to conquer the wicked enemy. Next morning, Eliezer revealed his dream and his master hastened to the king.

Eliezer's plan was successful. When peace was assured, the king summoned Eliezer. He gave him freedom, a fine manor for a home, and a princess to be his wife.

But Eliezer always stayed in his own rooms and wondered how he could escape. A voice from heaven, however, told him to wait. So each morning he went to bid the princess good day, and then retired to his own quarters.

Illustrated by Uri Shulevitz

Once the princess said angrily, "Why do you behave so strangely? I am your wife, yet you hardly speak to me!"

"Swear to keep my secret, and I will tell you," said Eliezer.

The princess took an oath, and Eliezer said, "Know then that I was captured by pirates in a distant land and sold as a slave. I have a dear wife in my own country. What is more, I am a Jew. You know the law of your land: no Jew may enter, under punishment of death."

That night the princess gave Eliezer much gold and secretly led him out of the city and he fled. On the way, bandits attacked him and robbed him of everything. Left alone in the middle of a dark forest, Eliezer wandered about until he spied a ray of light filtering through the trees. Then he beheld the figure of an old man with a white beard.

Eliezer recognized him. It was the Prophet Elijah.

"Do you see that narrow path?" Elijah said. "It will lead you out of the forest. There you will find a white horse waiting to take you home."

Eliezer followed the path, saw the horse, and rode swiftly over the mountains until he came to his inn at the riverbank. Waiting anxiously at the door was his wife Hannah, her arms spread wide in welcome.

A year later a son was born to them, and Eliezer named him Israel. Two years later Hannah died, leaving Israel alone with his father.

At the age of four, Israel knew the Bible, and his father began to study Talmud with him. When the boy was six, Eliezer called Israel to him and said, "My son, my time has come. I am about to die. I know that you will be a great light unto your people, and in heaven they speak of you already." With these words Eliezer closed his eyes and died.

Translated from the Yiddish by Morris Epstein

The Hole in the Bagels

ONCE THREE Helmites traveled to Vilna, to see what was going on in the outside world. The three were Shloime the scientist; Reuben the water-carrier; and Abba, the son of Gimpel, the Mayor.

In Vilna they went directly to a fine hotel. The next day they decided to divide the city into three sections. Each of them would explore one section thoroughly. After seven days they would meet again in the hotel to talk over their findings.

So they did. On the seventh day, the three Helmites reassembled, as planned, and sat down to their business. First spoke Reuben the water-carrier. "Brethren, the people of Vilna are stupid." Reuben reported. "I passed a cap-maker's shop and there was one cap I liked very much. I pointed it out to the owner of the shop. 'Why don't you buy it?' he asked. 'It's not expensive.' I told him, 'I'd like to buy it, but I'm embarrassed. I thought I had the measure of my head in my pocket, but I searched everywhere and I can't find it. I must have left it in Helm.'

"Well, the shopkeeper called in all the help and asked me to repeat what I had said. How they laughed! I stood there and wondered what all these fools of Vilna were laughing at."

Here Shloime picked up the story.

"Listen to this," he said. "I was standing in a bake shop, looking at something I liked. Then I heard a man say to a friend, 'Do you remember Benjamin, the son of Leibke, the shoemaker, who left Vilna fifteen years ago? He emigrated to London. Well, he left Vilna in a single pair of old, torn pants. Now he has a million!'

" 'You don't say; a cool million!'

" 'His father told me.'

"The other clucked his tongue. 'Some people are lucky.'

"I looked at them. What is there to envy, I ask you. The emigrant left with one pair of old, torn trousers and now he has a million old, torn pants. What will he do with a million torn and worthless pants? But I kept my peace. Besides, I was fascinated with what I saw in the bakery. I discovered something worth taking home, Look, I brought you some."

Shloime opened a small bag and took out twelve baked rings.

"What are those?" asked the others.

"They're called bagels."

"Bagels? That's a new one," said Abba.

"New or old," answered Shloime, "what difference does it make? Look at them! Did you ever see baked goods like this? It's the hole in the middle and a ring of dough around the hole. But never mind the shape. Taste it!"

They sampled the bagels. They smacked their lips and admitted that Shloime was right. The next day all three of them hurried to the bakery. They each ate a dozen bagels fresh from the oven, and found them still better, warm and crisp. When they could eat no more they said to the baker, "Please, baker, teach us how to bake bagels. We'll pay you handsomely for your trouble."

The baker agreed. He showed them how to knead the dough and how to cook the bagels in a big iron kettle, filled with boiling water. Then he taught them how to bake the

Illustrated by E. Schloss

boiled bagels on the floor of a hot brick oven.

They watched carefully, and then Reuben turned to Shloime, "I didn't grasp everything. Do you understand how to bake them?"

"I think so, but I'd like the baker to go over it again, from the beginning. Especially I'd like to know how he gets the hole in the middle."

The baker looked at them, and then asked quietly, "Are you from Helm, my brother Jews?"

They nodded.

"If that's the case, there's no point of going over the whole thing again. You surely grasped it all. As for the round hole in the center, that's simple. You take a ready-made hole, surround it with dough, join the ends, and there you have a bagel, ready to bake!"

Shloime was a bit ruffled. "Reb baker, I understood that the first time. My question is, where do you get the round holes?"

"Oh, that, my dear Helmites!" answered the baker. "I inherited a supply of round holes from my grandfather. I'm descended from generations and generations of bagel bakers. But as for your supply . . . Wait, let me look you over." He surveyed them. "You're sturdy fellows. You can each carry four strings of bagels on your neck, maybe even six, three dozen to the string. Eighteen dozen each comes to fifty-four dozen bagels. Fifty-four dozen bagels means six hundred and forty-eight holes. So you have a good supply of round holes from Vilna. All you have to do is to be careful to leave the hole intact when you eat the bagel, so it can be used again. If you sell a bagel, tell the customer not to destroy the hole. That way you'll have an endless supply of round holes."

Right then and there, the three Helmites decided to re-

turn home. Each one put six ropes of bagels around his neck, like a necklace. They put as many bagels as they could into their pockets to eat on the road.

It's quite a distance from Vilna to Helm. On the sixth day, as they approached Helm, the country became hilly and walking was more difficult. Two miles from Helm, they climbed a steep hill. Below it lay a village. Tired and perspiring, they sat down to rest. After a while, Shloime spoke.

"Abba and Reuben, don't be in a hurry to carry the bagels on your necks. Do you remember when we built our synagogue and couldn't carry the great log down the hill? We were told that any round object can be rolled down a

Illustrated by Bill Giacalone

hill. Do you remember?"

"Of course we remember!"

"Then let's take the bagels off the ropes and roll them down the hill!"

"That's a wonderful idea! Shloime, you have a head on your shoulders!"

They removed the ropes of the bagels from their necks, untied the strings, and rolled the bagels down the hill.

But no sooner did the bagels reach the valley than dogs and pigs from the village rushed out and made short work of them. When the Helmites saw what was happening, they shouted, "All right, eat all you want—but be careful with the holes! Watch out for the holes!"

But dogs are dogs, and pigs are pigs . . . when are they considerate? By the time the Helmites reached the foot of the hill, there was not a sign of a bagel, nor a trace of a round hole. Dogs are dogs and pigs are pigs . . . they have no idea of values.

Well, Shloime did not give in. He sat in lonely silence for seven weeks. He thought and figured, figured and thought, and with the help of a compass made circles on a baker's board. Then he showed the bakers how to ring the holes with dough. It took them a long time to learn to bake bagels without ready-made holes, but they managed.

Chuckles From Helm

THE SAGE WITH THE GOLDEN SHOES

THE CITIZENS of Helm had a council meeting. They decided that a community so famous for its wisdom should have a Chief Sage. So they elected a Chief Sage. To their dismay no one paid any attention to him, for when he walked in the street, he looked like any other Helm citizen.

So they bought him a pair of golden shoes.

The first day the Chief Sage put on his golden shoes a deep mud lay on the streets. The golden shoes got muddy, and no one paid any attention to the Chief Sage.

"If I don't get any attention," he complained, "I'll resign!"

"Right!" cried the Council. And they ordered a pair of fine leather shoes to be worn over the golden shoes.

But no one saw the gold under the leather, and again the Chief Sage was ignored.

So the Council ordered a pair of shoes with holes in them. But the mud went through the holes!

So they stuffed the holes with straw. The straw kept the

Illustrated by E. Schloss

181

mud out, but the golden shoes were hidden again.

"This is the last straw!" shouted the Chief Sage.

The Council agreed and held a solemn meeting. At last —a solution!

"From now on," they announced, "the Chief Sage will wear ordinary shoes. However, in order that everyone may know he is the Chief Sage, he will wear the golden shoes one on each hand!"

WHO NEEDS IT?

THE TOWN meetings in Helm debated only the most important matters. Once there was a discussion about the sun and the moon.

In the midst of it all, a Helmite arose. "Which, I ask you," he questioned, "is more important, the sun or the moon?"

Everyone turned to the Rabbi of Helm. He had the answer at once.

"The moon, of course," he declared. "It shines at night, when we need the light. As for the sun, why, it shines only during the day, when there is no need for it at all!"

ALL WET

A WISE MAN of Helm arose one summer day. "Nice weather," he mused. "I think I'll go for a swim."

He went down to the lake and stuck his toe in. "Ah! Just right."

He waded in until the water was over his head. "Glub!" he cried, as he went down once. "Glub! Glub!" he cried as he went down the second time.

There would have been no third time had other swimmers not come to his rescue.

As they dragged him dripping from the water, he raised his hand and swore solemnly, "Never, never will I go into the water until I learn how to swim!"

TOP SECRET

MERCHANTS of Helm often drove to nearby towns in order to sell their goods.

Once a Helm farmer drove to market in a neighboring town. As soon as he had come to a halt, he fed his bony

horse a skimpy handful of hay. He looked up and saw someone approaching.

"Aha!" he thought. "A customer already!"

He was right. The customer looked at the wagon, but it
was covered and he could not make out its contents.

He walked around to the driver and said, "Merchant,
what are you selling?"

The merchant from Helm bent over and whispered into
the customer's ear: "Oats."

"Oats!" cried the stranger in astonishment. "What's the
big secret about oats?"

"Please! Sh-h-h-!" begged the Helmite, with a swift
glance at his undernourished mare. "Don't say it loud. I
don't want my horse to know!"

JUSTICE IN HELM

HELM was darkened by sorrow and outrage. The town shoemaker had hit one of his customers over the head with a
hobnailed boot. The man had been killed instantly.

Justice moved swiftly in Helm. The shoemaker was
brought before the judge and the verdict was that the shoemaker must hang.

"Wait!" cried out a Helmite as the verdict was announced. "Have you new evidence?" asked the judge.

"No, your honor," said the Helmite. "But, if your honor
pleases, you have sentenced the town shoemaker. He's the
only one we've got. If you hang him, who will repair our
shoes?"

"True," said the judge. "I'll reconsider my verdict."

An hour later, he came out of his chambers. The Helmites gathered and he rapped his gavel for silence.

"Good people of Helm," he began, "the problem is a
weighty one. We have only one shoemaker. It would be a
wrong to the community to remove him. But a crime must

be punished. I say, let justice be served: since there are two tailors in Helm, let one of them be hanged instead!"

SCIENTIFIC EXPERIMENT

EVERYBODY in Helm was a sage. Naturally, each sage thought himself wiser than his fellow. So arguments and discussions were always under way, as sage tested sage for wisdom. Listen in on one such debate:

"Since you're so wise," said one sage to another, "try to answer this question: Why is it that when a slice of buttered bread falls to the ground, it always falls on the buttered side?"

"I'm not sure it does," replied the second sage. "I'm going to try it."

He brought a slice of bread and a pat of butter. He buttered the bread and dropped it. Lo! There was the butter, top side up!

"But see!" he cried in triumph. "The bread hasn't fallen

on its buttered side at all. What about your theory now?"

"Is that so!" laughed the other with a bit of a sneer. "You think you're smart, don't you! You buttered the bread on the wrong side, that's all!"

WELL PROTECTED

THE WISE MEN of Helm were always ready for any emergency. Once a pair of sages went for a stroll. One carried an umbrella, the other had none.

Suddenly it began to rain.

"Quick," said the sage without the umbrella. "Open your umbrella or we'll be soaked to the skin!"

"Ah," sighed the other. "It's no use. It won't help a bit."

"Why not?" sputtered the first sage, dripping wet. "It will protect us from the rain, won't it? That's what an umbrella is supposed to do, isn't it?"

"Yes," replied the umbrella-owner. "But this umbrella won't. It is as full of holes as Swiss cheese."

"Wh-a-at?" cried his companion. "Then why did you take it along in the first place?"

"That's easy," smiled the first wise man. "I didn't think it would rain."

III

The Bible as Background

King Agrippa and the First Fruits

BY S. SHIHOR

THE DEW glistened on the vine, and Uriel's hand trembled as he prepared to use the pruning knife. Would his Bikkurim be accepted?

Last year, when he was ten, his father had promised that he could join the Shavuot Bikkurim procession when he was one year older. Now the time had come. But Uriel would carry the basket without his father.

His father's vineyard belonged to someone else. Only one vine remained, and it was Uriel's.

Uriel knew just what to do. When his father was alive, he had gone with him to the vineyard to choose the ripest clusters. Father would tie them with a string and say, "These will be our Bikkurim—our First-Fruit Offering."

Uriel only had twelve bunches on his vine. He tied the finest. "This cluster is to be for Bikkurim," he repeated over and over again.

Uriel went into the house, and decorated his basket with dates and figs. The willow basket had three compartments. The Bikkurim were in the center; on each side was tied a white dove, a gift for the Kohanim, the priests.

When all was ready, his neighbor Haggai came to take Uriel along on his donkey. Uriel kissed his mother, and they joined the company of other travelers who were going to Jerusalem.

Uriel's village of Avihiel was a small one, but its Bikkurim caravan was beautiful. The ox that led the procession was large and strong, with gilded horns and a crown of olives on his head.

Elimelekh, the oldest inhabitant, rode behind the ox. He

turned to Haggai, saying, "There is no need to hurry. We will arrive at our post when day is done. In the torchlight our caravan will appear the finest of all."

The "posts" were cities near Jerusalem where the pilgrims gathered just before Shavuot. At daybreak they proceeded to Jerusalem without confusion or crowding. The post assigned to Uriel's village was the city of Betar.

In the afternoon the caravan reached the Orchard of Pomegranates. The orchard-keeper welcomed the travelers. The pilgrims gratefully fanned out under the trees and quenched their thirst with cooling drinks offered by the owner of the orchard.

After lunch the elders lay down to nap, but the younger people started to dance. Only when the sun had set did the caravan continue on its journey to Betar. The torches were lit, and the procession wound its way through the mountains.

The inhabitants of Betar spread out mats for the guests, and again the youth from all the communities that gathered in Betar danced and sang far into the night.

At dawn Uriel was abruptly awakened by a cry: "Children of Israel, pilgrims of the Post of Betar, arise and let us go to Zion!"

Rubbing the sleep from their eyes, the pilgrims took their baskets and formed caravans again. At the head of each caravan marched the flute-players, and drummers walked at the sides.

At the gate of Jerusalem, a committee came out to meet them and formed two rows on both sides of the gate. When it was the turn of Uriel's caravan to enter, the citizens of Jerusalem cried in the ancient way of greeting the pilgrims, "Our brothers from the village of Avihiel, enter the city of Zion in peace!"

In answer, the drums beat and the flutes played, and the procession entered Jerusalem with rhythmical dancing. At the Temple each man lifted his basket and put it on his shoulder, and the chief singer of the village chanted: "Praise God in His Temple. . ." until they reached the Temple Court and they heard the voices of the choir of Levites.

Uriel's heart beat faster as he gripped the basket and raised it to his shoulder. They moved into the Temple Court in single file. The Kohanim were in the aisles, ready to receive the Bikkurim. Louder and louder sang the Levite choir, and the sound of musical instruments was heard from the Temple.

A whisper rippled through the crowd. "Here comes Agrippa! Here comes the king!"

Uriel saw the king.

Agrippa was dressed in a cloak of dazzling white. His golden crown was on his head, and on his shoulder he bore a Bikkurim basket made of beaten gold.

Uriel wondered aloud, "Does the king carry the Bikkurim by himself?"

"That's right, my son," whispered Haggai. "Even the king must fulfill the mitzvot, the laws of our Torah."

All at once, a resounding cry burst from the throats of the great assembly of pilgrims. It echoed again and again, drowning the voices of the Levite choir, "Long live Agrippa our king!"

Now it was the turn of Haggai and Uriel to enter the Temple Court. The king was still approaching.

"Do as I do!" Haggai whispered. With both hands, he lifted the basket from his shoulder and gave it to the priest, saying: "Behold, I have brought the first of the fruit of the land." And soon as Haggai finished, Uriel started to do the same.

"How old are you, my child?" the priest inquired.

"Eleven," said Uriel.

The priest patted Uriel's head and smiled. "You are too young. The Torah does not require you to bring Bikkurim. I cannot accept them from you."

Uriel grew very sad. The happy holiday feeling which had filled his heart disappeared. His eyes brimmed with tears.

"Please, dear Kohen," he pleaded. "My father died but five months ago. His last words were, 'Uriel, do not forget to bring Bikkurim in from the vineyard.' But things went badly, and my mother was forced to sell the vineyard."

"Then the vineyard is not yours," said the priest. "And Bikkurim, you know, must be brought from one's own land."

"But this branch, O Kohen, is mine," cried Uriel. "The day we sold the vineyard I uprooted this vine and planted it in our yard. The elders of our town told me that it is my vine, and the First Fruits must be taken from it! I did everything to fulfill my father's last wish, everything, and now you forbid me. . ."

Illustrated by Dan Gelbart

A choking feeling in his throat stopped the flow of Uriel's words. Big tears splashed on his beautiful cluster of grapes. The pair of doves blinked at him. Everyone turned to look at him. Even the priest brushed away a tear. "Wait, my child," he said. "I will ask the opinion of the older Kohanim. This has never happened before."

Then Uriel heard a deep, soft voice at his side. King Agrippa was standing next to him.

"Do not cry, boy. As king of Israel I return to you the vineyard which belonged to your father. From now on it is yours. The man who owns it now will be paid from the king's treasury. Kohen! Accept the child's Bikkurim."

Uriel looked up gratefully at King Agrippa. He lifted his basket, gave it to the priest and turned to bow down to the king. Instead, King Agrippa stopped and lifted Uriel into his arms.

"Do not bow before a man of flesh and blood," he said. "Although I am king, remember that you stand in the House of Almighty God, King of Kings!"

Uriel buried his head in the folds of the king's robe and wept with happiness.

The Revolt

BY FRIEDA CLARK HYMAN

I AM MICA, son of Mephibosheth, of the House of Kish. King David restored our land to my father. And he appointed Ziba and his household to serve us. He also insisted that my father and I eat at the king's own table.

Still, my father frowns as I go to the king in the cool of the evening. Not that my father has forbidden me to enter the royal terraces. And in truth why should he? For my lord David is more than my king. He is a beloved teacher, who instructs me on the harp and the pipe. From him I have learned the gentle songs of the shepherd, the sighing melodies of the trees, the mysterious call of the wind and the stars. Yes, during many a twilight hour he has told me of his own nights as a shepherd lad, when the sheep stirred only in their sleep, and a single jackal wailed between the rocks. When in the rustle of the tree tops he seemed to hear the footsteps of Almighty God.

King David and I are of different tribes. He is of Judah, and I am from Benjamin. But once he called me son, his own beloved grandson, and he kissed me on the forehead. Everyone knows how much King David loves his sons. To be cailed son by him is the most precious gift he could offer me.

Surely I should be the happiest of all youths. But my joy can never be complete. My father, you see, cannot use his legs.

It happened this way. My great-grandfather Saul was the first King of Israel. He died on Mount Gilboa fighting the Philistines with three of his sons. Among them was Jonathan, my father's father.

When the people heard of this dreadful defeat they fled.

My father's nurse dropped Mephibosheth in her flight. The fall crippled him for life.

From the way my father sits in his chair, he might have been a mighty warrior. His chest is deep, and his shoulders are wide. On horseback he is like all men. I have seen my father mount his horse from his chair through the power of his mighty shoulders.

Every morning it is our custom to ride forth, my father on his stallion and I on a colt. First we go down into the valley, through the fields of ripening fruits and grains, then out farther into the hills of Judea, and always up on some craggy height.

That is the moment I like best with my father. Then all the bitter lines seem to fade from his face as he lifts his head to the sun and shows me the landmarks of our country. From him I learn of the great wars and heroes of my people. Up there, my father points to where Samson came from Dan and destroyed the Philistines—one thousand of them, my father says, and all slain with the jawbone of an ass. And there in Ephraim rose Deborah and the faint-hearted Barak to destroy the power of Sisera. And then he tells of the other famous leaders, till my blood quickens with excitement and glory.

But always, at the end, he speaks of Saul. As though all these judges and heroes were but the rungs on the ladder which lead to the throne of my great-grandfather, Saul.

Tall and handsome Saul had been, yet humble and modest when he was chosen king.

"Father," I often pleaded, "tell me of Jabesh-gilead."

Mephibosheth did not have to be asked twice.

"Ammon was the enemy," he began. "Nahash was their king. And he encamped against the city of Jabesh-gilead." He paused and frowned: "He was the victor."

"Not yet," I cried.

"It was only a matter of time. The men of Jabesh-gilead knew it, so they sued for a peace treaty. And Nahash agreed."

"That was not a treaty," I protested. "That insult!"

"It was." My father's face had set into iron lines. "The right eye was what Nahash demanded. The right eye of every man of Jabesh-gilead. The dog! And they would have had to agree if it weren't for. . ."

"Saul!" I sang out the golden name.

"Saul." Mephibosheth's eyes were two suns. "*There* was a man. A real ruler of Israel. Not one who sends others to do his fighting."

I did not respond to this taunt at King David, undeserved though it was. "Father," I cried, "did Saul save Jabesh-gilead?"

"He did." But thoughts of King David had curled his lips with bitterness. He pounded his gloved hand upon the saddle. The stallion reared and bolted down the hill. I

Illustrated by W.T. Mars

could do nothing but follow after.

It was on such a day some weeks later that this story begins. The haze over the orchards and vines, the humming of the bees and flash of a bird's wing in the golden air gave little hint of the tragedy which was to unfold on that day.

As always, my father and I were on one of the small spurs of Judea, and as always my father was speaking of the deeds of Saul.

"Father," I asked, drowsy with the sun on my back, "you never speak of my grandfather Jonathan. Was he not as great a warrior as Saul?"

To my horror, my father's face became red and dark with fury. "I did not know my father," he said. "I was five years old when he fell in battle. I knew nothing of him. Nothing." I knew from that awful anger I must not ask on. I pointed to the sun.

"It is late, father. The sun is almost directly over us."

"And we must not keep the king waiting," my father mocked as he always did when he spoke of David.

"It would be discourteous, my lord father," I replied meekly.

"Never mind, Mica," my father said harshly. "You will not have to be so courteous for long." And to himself he added, "After today."

I could feel my heart against my ribs. "What does my lord father mean?" I whispered.

"Absalom, the king's own son," my father began, then caught himself. "But there," he smiled a bitter smile, "You are one of King David's men. Is that not so, Mica?"

I raised two tear-filled eyes. "We are all his men, father," I pleaded. He is so good to . . ." I hesitated, "to me."

My father's brows drew together, dark and foreboding. "Because he had stolen your throne, Mica?" He bent over his saddle towards me.

"MY throne?" I stammered.

"Whose else? It belonged to your great-grandfather, to my father, to me! Yes, to me! And to you!"

"No, my father," I begged. "Do not SAY THIS. King David is our king. All Israel knows this."

"Even in Hebron?" And Mephibosheth laughed loudly.

"Hebron is part of Israel too."

"Yes, it is; that it is," my father fairly shouted as he pointed his mount towards Jerusalem. "Hebron is the true Israel today." And with the wild cry, "Hebron, Hebron!" trailing behind him like a crimson banner, he spurred his stallion down the hill, and up the road that led to home. And to the king.

*   *   *

The warriors and courtiers awaiting King David in the long dining hall were as quiet as statues. It was Joab, King David's Commander-in-Chief, who finally spoke. "Absalom is in Hebron." He fairly spat the words.

A chill gripped my bones. Hebron! The true Israel, Mephibosheth had cried.

"And sent there by my own master," Joab's lips tightened.

"What harm, Joab, is there in Hebron for us?" Zadok the priest asked. "Absalom has but gone to fulfill a vow he made there."

At my side my father, Mephibosheth, chuckled. Only it was not a happy chuckle. I shuddered. My father really did hate the king. King David, whom I loved so much.

"By heaven," Joab was saying, "it is a vow to seize the crown."

"Careful, Joab!" Zadok warned.

"No, Israel must be careful."

"He is not king yet. Even if he seeks the crown."

"But he will be if David does not bestir himself. Men have been flocking to Hebron from all over Israel. The famine we have had has not only shrunk their bellies, but their minds as well."

"There have always been discontented fools in the world."

"Do you call Ahitophel a fool?"

Ahitophel. A sigh escaped every lip. The wisest man of Israel. David's closest adviser. Ahitophel with Absalom? Then God have pity on us all.

I turned to my father. And there, as I feared, I saw the wild, bitter joy. I could have thrown myself upon my father, pleading with him, but it was, I knew, impossible. Just then a servant appeared in the archway.

"His majesty the king!"

The king had not been well, and gray streaked his beard and hair. Nevertheless he stood upright before us, his large black eyes melting the chill in the room.

"My apologies, my lords." The king bowed graciously. "But the hours speed by when one is working."

Joab made a queer noise, and I knew immediately the king had been busy with poems and lyrics. The service of the Temple which was yet to be built was the chief concern these days. I had learned most of his compositions by heart.

The king was now at the table. From the board he took a loaf of bread, and breaking it into a score of pieces, he said the blessing. The pages ran with the pieces of bread so that all might eat of the king's personal bounty. Then we were seated.

The king was particularly lighthearted. His eyes sparkled, and his fingers tapped constantly upon the board, as though they itched from the strings. Finally it was evident he could not contain himself.

Only the sound of chewing was heard. Then David said, "My harp!" and the instrument was brought to him.

"Mica," the king said. My heart leaped.

"My lord king." I was upon my feet immediately.

"Come nearer to me. You shall sing while I play upon my harp. There is nothing so pleasing to the stomach as sweet music." Teasingly, he turned to Joab at his right. "Is it not so, my lord Joab?"

The Commander-in-Chief had paled. Pounding upon the table, he arose and cried: "No, Sire! My ears cannot listen to the melody of the harp!"

The king's light smile froze. "To what melody can my lord Joab's ears attend?" he asked icily.

"To the horns, your Majesty. To the horns of war! You are in danger, King David."

"I think not." The king was trying desperately not to be aroused. "Ammon is subdued," the king said, "Moab crushed, Edom, Aram, Philistia . . . No, I must disagree with you, my lord Joab. Your great love for us bids you to see war where there is peace."

"The enemy is within, Sire."

Was I mistaken, or did I see the king's eyes light upon my father?

"I see no enemy here," the king was saying.

"The enemy," Joab replied slowly, "is in Hebron."

"Joab!" The king started to rise, and for a second we feared he might draw his sword. Instead he sank back into his chair. "I know," he said with an effort, "who is in Hebron. Prince Absalom."

"With half of Jerusalem following him." The king grew tense. "With men streaming to Hebron from all the four corners of the land!" Joab continued relentlessly.

The king was white. "With certain elders, and—" Joab paused, bending his bold glance upon King David "—and Ahitophel."

"No!" the king cried.

"But yes."

The king bent forward over the table as we all watched with bated breath. We waited silently and saw the king slowly stand straight again. The weakness had passed. His eyes once more shone, the muscles of his face relaxed.

"Joab, Joab," the king chuckled. "You are forgiven."

"My lord?" Joab stared helplessly.

"If Ahitophel is with the young man, then he has surely gone to pay his vow. Ahitophel is my own wise counselor. Would he let the prince act recklessly?"

"Ahitophel has deserted you."

Now the king's eyes were alight with the pride of a father. "Joab, you were ever suspicious. Ask of the others." He pointed to his company. "Who else accuses my son of treason?" The king cast a regal eye the length of the table. Did he linger at my father's chair? Again I could not be sure. But no one stirred, though a few heads hung low, unable to meet the king's inspection. "You see, Joab," he said triumphantly. "No one. No one but you."

"Their loyalty has fled before their fear." It was Joab's turn to inspect the table, and this he did with haughty and contemptuous eyes. "They think that by keeping the truth from you, they will hurt you less. But they are fools, fools and cowards."

The king picked up his harp. But before he could pluck one string Joab turned with a mighty curse, and was about to stride out of the dining hall.

"TEKIAH!"

The wild blast of the horn stiffened us all. Now the sound of running feet grew stronger and stronger until the messenger, dusty and weary, burst through the archway.

"Absalom is crowned King in Hebron," he called from a parched throat. "Twenty thousand have joined his ranks. Ahitophel stands at his right side!"

Instantly there was a mighty shuffling of chairs. But Joab was already in command. "To your troops!" he called. "All arms in readiness. Abishai, Ittai, raise the standards! Blow the horns! Summon every loyal man. For David and for Israel!"

And as this company rushed to and fro the king bent forward upon his arms. Down the board Mephibosheth, my father, sat watching the king with the cruel eyes of a hungry tiger. My place was at my father's side; but my feet would not move from the king. I bent at his side and heard between the sobs of an old man, the pathetic moan, "Absalom, Absalom. How could you, Absalom? Absalom, oh my son, how could you?"

*　*　*

Later that day I approached my father. I had made up my mind. I wore my darkest tunic, and at my side hung my small sword.

"Father"—I bowed—"all is ready."

"Ready, Mica?" Mephibosheth's forehead wrinkled. "Ready for what?"

"For leaving Jerusalem."

"And where are we going?"

"Where?" It was my turn to question. "Where but with the army? With King David!"

Mephibosheth's eyes narrowed. "And what makes you so sure we go with the king?"

"But what else," I stammered. "We are of the king's household."

"We, princes of the house of Kish?" Mephibosheth's scorn was undisguised.

"We ate at the king's table these many years."

"Foolish child," my father said pityingly. "Where else should King David keep a son of Saul but where he could watch him?"

"No, my father." I gathered my courage and raised my eyes to him. "The king keeps us at his table out of his love for us."

Mephibosheth darkened. "Love," he cursed the word. "It made a traitor of my father. Shall it do the same to you?"

I stepped back. To call his father Jonathan a traitor! That prince who had given his life for his country! I shook my head in wonder and disbelief.

"And you do not believe it, Mica?" My father was clutching at the arms of his chair.

"I cannot believe my grandfather Jonathan was a traitor."

"What then is he who gives up his throne, yes, conspires to give it up to this son of Jesse? What then is he who betrays his own father?"

"No, no," I gasped. "It cannot be."

"But it was. Did he not send away his father's enemy? Send this very David away though he knew he would seize Saul's throne at the first opportunity? And for what"—Mephibosheth paused—"but his love for David?"

What could I do? What could I say? I had already made up my mind to beg the king to take me as his armor-bearer. Yes, even though I knew my father would object. Well, there was only one more argument left. I had prepared it for this refusal.

"Father," I began, "what will happen when the king returns?"

"Absalom has fifty thousand men. Now, consider. Do you think David will return?"

"And when Absalom"—I almost choked on the name—"sits on the throne? Will it be any better for you? For us?"

"If he sits on the throne," my father corrected me. "Do you think Ahitophel has striven for Absalom? No, Mica. If the house of Jesse be destroyed, to whom shall Israel turn, Mica?"

"You do not mean," I gasped, "you cannot . . ."

"Why not? Is not the house of Kish the true royal house of Israel? On whom more fitting does the crown rest?"

I did not dare remind my father of his folly. Joab would not accept such a one as my father for his commander. Even my father knew Saul had been chosen partly, if not mainly, for his huge and manly figure.

I turned away to the window of this room that faced the Mount of Olives. Not that I craved the countryside, but rather to collect my thoughts, to choose the gentlest words. For I had to accompany David. With Ziba here, my father would manage. And I would not feel as though I deserted

him. But before I could speak, I beheld the king climbing the Mount. He was barefoot, and his head was covered, while behind him there followed a band, all with heads covered and barefoot. Though I could not hear them, I knew they were weeping. Then suddenly, to my amazement, our own servant Ziba appeared leading two asses laden with bundles.

"Father," I cried out.

"What is it, Mica? What do you see?"

"Ziba! He is talking to the king. And he is giving him gifts." I tried to keep the joy out of my voice.

"So he has done it," my father muttered. "The dog said he would bring them to the king. Two hundred loaves of my good bread, clusters of raisins, summer fruits, wine. And after I forbade it. Warned him!" There was a pause, and then the threat filled the room. "He'll pay with his skin."

I made no reply. There was no use in further protest. "He is pointing downward, Father," I remarked for want of anything else. "At us, I think."

Mephibosheth laughed bitterly. "Let him," he said. "Let him tell what he wishes. His day is over. Mine, yours, shall now begin. Yes, now I shall avenge myself for the evil David has done unto the house of Kish."

A cloud darkened the scene before me. I knew I could never leave Mephibosheth. For if Ziba had turned against my father, who would stand by him? There was no other choice for me. If I joined the king, I might be slaying my father. What son could take such guilt upon himself? Even for my beloved King David.

But if my father's charge were true, my grandfather Jonathan had done exactly that. I turned back to Mephibosheth. He was watching me sharply. Was his charge true? Had Jonathan betrayed his own father Saul for David? God of my fathers, would I ever know? Could I?

It was at this moment that Jared, Ziba's eldest son, entered. He was a thin, middle-aged man, small and bent with the work of the fields. But now his dislike for my father held him erect.

"You are cast out, Mephibosheth," he declared. "The king has taken away your property."

"For Ziba, no doubt," my father sneered.

"For Ziba." Jared did not flinch.

"Then enjoy it while you can, O son of Ziba," my father said. "For it shall not be for long."

"An ingrate must reap the ingrate's harvest."

"Crow not so soon, you cock," my father growled. "The battle is not joined."

"Either way," Jared replied, "you are undone."

My father whitened. And I as well. The meaning was too clear.

"So he has ordered my death," my father said.

"Do you speak of the king?" Jared seemed to grow before our eyes. "No, he has not commanded this for you. You know you are safe. Or have you forgotten you are Jonathan's son?"

"No," Mephibosheth cried as one stung. "I have never forgotten, nor shall I."

"Of that I can be sure." Jared replied. "You have taken advantage of its power all these years. You knew too well how Jonathan protected you."

And even as he spoke, I sought the meaning of these words. For surely Jonathan was dead. Fallen in battle a hero. Then how could he protect my father or anyone?

I could not ask Jared. Ziba and his vast family were now my enemy as well as my father's. Mephibosheth would never explain. And King David? King David was far from me as well. He had disappeared down the other side of the Mount of Olives.

*   *   *

Today or tomorrow, perhaps the house of Jonathan comes to an end. My father, Mephibosheth, was Jonathan's only son. And I am Mephibosheth's only son. We two, my father and I, are branded traitors.

It will make no difference that I am innocent. The king will have no choice but to punish us both. And despite Jared's assurance, what punishment can we expect but death?

Absalom is dead, slain by Joab. Absalom's commander-in-chief is dead, also slain by Joab. Ahitophel has taken his own life. The forest where the battle raged now conceals twenty thousand corpses. Israel, with the exception of my own tribe, Benjamin, is united behind David.

There will be still another battle before Benjamin is subdued. But in the meantime we shall be here awaiting the king.

I have not seen my father except to bring him bread and

to attend to his other needs. We are like two strangers, he and I. It is queer how old I feel now.

My father is so alone now. His hair, I have noticed, he has left uncombed. His beard he has not trimmed. Out of pity I have tried to brush his hair, to wash his feet, but he has refused. He will take nothing from me but food.

So he sits in his room, and I in mine, waiting. The king has just returned to his palace. Well, we shall have deserved our fate. No king was kinder than was David to me and my father.

I rise. There is a knocking from my father's room. I hasten to him.

"Mica," my father commands me, "saddle the horses."

I shake my head sadly. "It is too late, father," I whisper.

"Saddle the horses, Mica." Again that command. "We go to welcome the king."

Did I hear correctly? Was my father impatient for his punishment? Would he face the lion in the hour of his victory? "The king?" I repeated. "King David?"

"Has Absalom been victorious?" my father asked impatiently. "Of course, King David. We must go like loyal citizens to greet our triumphant leader."

I could not look at my father. What manner of man was this? Almost I preferred him as he was in his fury, yes, in his wild and unreasoning hatred. There, at least, was a man. But this deceit! It was more than I could bear.

"No," I cried, "no, we did not go to him then. We shall not go to him today, come what may."

"Would you hand your father over to death? The king will never harm you—only me."

"Perhaps he will spare us," I said weakly.

My father looked at me, and I could not deny him.

"I shall bring the horses," I said, and left for the stables.

And so it was that Mephibosheth ben Jonathan, haggard and unkempt upon his horse, and I, his son, went forth to greet the king. It was but a stone's throw, but with no Ziba to help, we had to go by horse.

I saw David even before our horses started up. He was pacing back and forth upon his terrace. He was gray, and stooped with suffering.

He halted, hearing the hooves of our mounts, and raised his head to us as we approached. Before I could say a word, my father had flung himself from his saddle and lay stretched out before the king. But the king, I noticed, had stiffened. My spirits sank. Whatever hope I had clung to, vanished.

"Why did you not go with me, Mephibosheth?" King David asked icily.

"My lord, O king, my servant deceived me, for my servant said, I will saddle me a donkey that I may ride thereon and go with the king; because, as you know, your servant is lame."

"Not too lame, Mephibosheth, to mount the horse."

"Ah, I see," my father cried. "Ziba has slandered me to you. But my lord the king is an angel of God. Do therefore what is good in your eyes. For all my father's house was deserving of death at the hand of the king." My father, bent to the ground, did not see the quiver that passed through the king. I wanted to cry out to him, to warn him, but my lips were sealed, both for fear and for shame. "Yet," Mephibosheth continued, "did you set your servant among them and he did eat at your own table. What right have I, or why should I cry any more unto the king?"

"Then have done," the king thundered, and my father's head jerked up. "You have come to me in the slyness of your heart, Mephibosheth, but you have never fooled me. Do I not know how all these years you sat at my board, plotting and planning to destroy me? It is so. Do not deny it."

My father had hoisted himself to his knees somehow. It was all over, he so clearly realized. And indeed what else could he or anyone think? There was no more to be gained by cunning. The true Mephibosheth glared back at the king.

"But you kept me near to you, did you not? You feared Mephibosheth, feared the son of Saul."

For a moment there was a dreadful silence. Then the king cried, "Feared you. *You,* Mephibosheth?"

I squirmed for my father. The meaning was too clear. At that point I almost hated David.

Mephibosheth stared back at the king defiantly. A strange pride filled my being. "Yes, me. Say it. Me, the cripple." Mephibosheth flung his words at David. "But crippled or not, I am a king's son. I am the grandson of Saul."

"In your suspicions. But not in your meanness." David shook his head sadly. "For Saul was a man, noble and open like the mountains of Judea."

"A man who hated you." Mephibosheth's tongue was a piercing arrow.

"When the madness gripped him"—and a shadow seemed to settle over the king. "But otherwise he loved me. And I loved him. As I loved"—and the king's voice sank to a whisper,—"as I loved your own father."

"That traitor!"

The word was barely past his lips when the king was upon him, his sword poised. Forgetful of all, I threw myself between my father and my king. "Slay me," I cried. "Slay me instead!" And I waited for the plunge of the blade.

An eternity passed. Then I was within the king's arms.

"No, you are my child, my beloved child," the king said. "You are Jonathan whom I love. All of him I can behold in you. Blessed are you, Mica, who has brought the dear presence of Jonathan back to me." And he rocked me in his arms back and forth. Finally he remembered Mephibosheth.

"Behold," David said to him, "you cannot love; here is love which has restored your life unto you. Here you see why I have set you at my table. Not for you, but for him who was your father and my brother. He who was the most loyal, yes, the bravest of Israel.

"Now take your son and return unto your house. I shall not break my vow I made unto Jonathan. Only your possessions shall be divided between you and Ziba. As for the boy, when he reaches manhood, I shall provide for him, so that he shall not suffer for his father's sins."

And now, between David and me, we mounted Mephibosheth upon his horse, and slowly returned home. But for all of the shame, my heart was no longer weighed down. For now I knew the bond that had united Jonathan and David. Now I knew the evil that hatred creates, and the wonders that can be wrought by sincere friendship and true love.

The Bush

BY MENAHEM STERN

IN AN oasis, amid tall and beautiful trees, grew a frail bush. The leaves on its thin branches were few and dry and its fruit was puny and stunted.

Wandering Bedouins who used to stop in the oasis plucked the fruit from the well-nourished trees, ate heartily, and rested in the cool shade of their fragrant boughs. But to the small, frail bush no one came. Yet the hot desert breezes did not pass it by. The cruel winds beat against the bush with all their might in an effort to uproot it.

The young tree, aware of its weakness and skimpy size, felt downhearted and asked:

"Why am I the frailest of all bushes and trees in the oasis? What have I done that my lot is so hard?"

"That's how things are in this world," harshly answered the big trees. And after their answer the bush felt even more melancholy than before.

One day a searching tongue of fire descended from the sky and enveloped the bush. The young bush was terrified. It rustled its branches and called out in despair:

"Now I am lost! Fire is more destructive than the desert wind, more painful than loneliness, more shameful than dry branches. The fire will put an end to me!"

Then the fire lit up with a brightness which was greater than the brightness of the sun. It spoke:

"Do not fear, bush, for I am not the fire which consumes. I am the fire of the eternal God, the God of love and mercy. And soon you will see and hear things which no tree on earth has ever seen or heard."

The young bush wanted to say something but it was un-

212

able to utter a word, for it was filled with awe. It could only bow deeply, and brush the ground with low-hanging branches.

Then, through the thin veil of glowing flame, it looked about with curiosity.

At the foot of a hill a shepherd was grazing a flock of sheep. The bush saw the shepherd stare in surprise and in wonder, for the fire was burning ceaselessly, and yet the bush was not consumed.

The shepherd left his flock and came closer and the bush could see his keen-eyed, marveling face and his jaw hanging slack with amazement.

Illustrated by E. Schloss

At this instant the voice of God spoke from the fire, saying:

"Moses! Moses! Take off your shoes, for the ground on which you stand is holy."

"How miraculous!" whispered the bush. "Not once in all my life have I experienced an event like this. And who could have known that the soil on which I grow is holy ground?" And again the bush bowed low.

The bush grew quickly silent as the Lord's voice again spoke to the shepherd, telling him to go to Pharaoh, the ruler of Egypt, and order him to let the children of Israel free.

When Moses had left, the Lord spoke again from the crackling fire. This time He spoke to the bush:

"You have found grace in My eyes, and therefore have you seen and heard Me as I spoke to My faithful servant Moses. Rejoice in your lot, bush, and let no blazing desert sun, sweeping sandstorm nor weakness of branches trouble you."

And as the Lord finished speaking the great flame disappeared.

From that day on the bush was content with its lot, for it knew that it had fulfilled a great mission in the history of the world.

Foolish Balaam and the Wise Donkey

BY MENAHEM STERN

BALAAM rode his donkey to the plain on which the Israelites had camped. He intended to curse them, but God gave the animal wisdom and taught it the knowledge of right and wrong.

The donkey thought sadly:

"My master is looked upon as a wise man and a prophet, but he is really weak in character, for he was easily persuaded by Balak, king of Moab, to do a wicked deed. What Balaam wants to do to the Hebrew people, who are proceeding peacefully towards their Promised Land, is a cruel thing.

"I will therefore take him through a lovely part of the countryside, and when he sees the beauty of the hills and the valleys which God has created, Balaam will also think of God's goodness and will not agree to Balak's wicked plan of cursing the Hebrews."

So the good, gentle donkey took a road which led through some very graceful countryside.

It was springtime. A light blue sky arched over the valleys

Illustrated by Bill Giacalone

and hills, over the fruit-laden almond, fig and pomegranate trees. When a breeze blew through the air, a rain of petals fell from the blooming trees, as if they longed for the earth from which the trees grew and were nourished.

The fragrant scent of spring and earth, mingled with the tender smell of blossoms, filled the air. On a nearby tree, a bird sang with a sweet but sad voice. The bird was happy because spring had arrived, bringing with it much beauty and loveliness. At the same time the songster seemed to be sad, perhaps because the blossoms were already falling off the trees.

The bird's song was so gentle and delicate that it almost moved the sensitive donkey to tears.

"I am only a donkey and not as wise as man, yet I can feel the glory of the Lord, who in His kindness created all that is beautiful and good to all my senses. I wish that my master felt the same way, so that he could hate no one. Then only friendliness and love would live in his heart," thought the wise and sensitive donkey.

But Balaam was busy thinking of himself, dreaming of the handsome rewards and honors which the warlike Moabite king would give him after he had performed his wicked deed.

It was a warm day, and as the donkey carried Balaam through a village it saw a young man rolling away a huge stone which covered the village well, so that the older men and women standing nearby and waiting eagerly for water might be able to drink.

The donkey, seeing this, thought hopefully:

"I will let my master know that I am thirsty, and when he goes to bring me water he will see how people can be kind to each other. Perhaps that will change him for the better and he will not carry out Balak's plan."

The donkey brayed with a shrill voice, thus announcing its urgent need for water.

But Balaam, instead of bringing water for the donkey, kicked and whipped the well-meaning animal and went on dreaming of wealth and power. With a heavy heart the donkey gave up the idea of improving its master, and regretfully thought about the Israelites who would soon be hurt by Balaam's sharp-tongued curses and thus become an easy prey for Moab's attack.

God pitied the donkey and sent His angel to stand before Balaam with a drawn sword. And, as the Bible tells us, Balaam's plans were changed. The good donkey's hopes came true at last. As Balaam stood on the hill overlooking the orderly Israelite camp, he blessed the Hebrews instead of cursing them.

The Cedar's Surprise

BY MARIE CAMPBELL

AGAINST the background of majestic, snow-capped mountains, the lofty cedar of Lebanon lifted its wide, flat boughs in worship of God, its creator. Cool breezes blowing through the spacious branches caused the egg-shaped cones hanging from the cedar to sway in gentle rhythm, to and fro. Full forty feet around and many times as high, the straight, strong trunk stood firmly with its long, curving roots deeply planted in the rich, moist earth.

Proud and devoted, the mighty cedar made an earnest declaration.

"I shall serve God with my beauty and my strength!"

The bright green needles fluttered in approval of such a

worthy purpose, and the cedar swayed slightly, sending its fragrance into the air. For a moment it was happy and satisfied, but soon it realized there was no one near to appreciate its efforts. What good was the beauty and fragrance without someone to enjoy it?

"I could serve God better if I were also helping humanity," mused the cedar.

Whispering to the birds that perched upon its branches, the cedar made an urgent plea.

"Fly away, my little feathered friends, to the dwellings of men and speak of my grandeur. Bid them hasten hither to observe my glory."

Obediently they took flight and winged their way to sing to mankind of the splendor of the cedar.

A few days later the tall tree looked over the branches of the other trees and beheld a group of men toiling up the mountainside.

"Ah," he murmured in satisfaction. "Here they come now to gaze upon my beauty!"

The cedar breathed deeply of the fresh mountain air and lifted its branches high, stretching itself to its full height, impatiently awaiting their admiration.

Struck by the noble sight, the men stopped suddenly and turned aside to examine the tree closely. Passing their hands over the rough, reddish-brown bark flecked with white, they looked up from the base into the branches, noting the straight line of the cedar.

"This one will do," one of the men said sharply. "Get to work on it."

Great saws were brought forth and placed against the large trunk, and the toothed edge began to sink into the coarse bark and tear it painfully.

"What are you doing to me?" asked the tree in terror. "I

have not harmed you!"

If the men heard, they paid no attention. After much effort, they succeeded in cutting through the trunk. Bewildered, the mighty tree swayed back and forth and finally crashed to the ground with a great thud. It lay there helpless, sobbing desperately.

"Why, oh why, was I not content to shelter the birds and beasts of the field, instead of seeking man's admiration!" it wondered bitterly.

The men began to move among its many branches with shining sharp-edged axes. Speechless with new horror, the cedar watched them swing their tools and chop away its

Illustrated by Bill Giacalone

branches. It was not enough that they had felled it and brought it low to the ground. Now they were robbing it of his green-needled cloak! All of its beauty was rapidly vanishing! At last it lay there, a great bare log without even a single branch.

Next, the men moved along the length of the tree trunk, prying the bark loose.

"Oh! Oh!" the cedar cried out. "Do you strip me even of my bark?"

Indeed, they were doing just that. Bare and quivering, it lay exposed without a trace of its former power and glory.

"There is nothing more they can do to me," mourned the cedar.

But he was wrong. He was tied with heavy chains and ropes and hauled down the mountain to a sawmill. There they sliced him into many planks. These planks were sanded and polished until the cedar thought he could stand the ordeal no longer. Raw and sore from all the scraping and sanding, he gained a short rest from the hands of men. For many weeks, he lay in the hold of a ship as it sailed down the Mediterranean Sea.

As he was being unloaded at Joppa, he almost forgot his grief in the interest of new surroundings. For the first time in his life he gazed upon civilization. He wondered what part he was to play here. Perhaps a useful life awaited him where no one would know of his previous splendor. Slowly, he was becoming used to his lot when he began another journey.

Placed upon carts pulled by oxen, he began to move upland to Jerusalem, about twenty-five miles distant. There he was delivered into the hands of more men who began a new process. A thick, sticky substance was smeared upon him from head to foot. Not even bothering to watch, he listened aimlessly to the buzz of voices about him. Suddenly, his ears picked up. They were discussing him.

"Is this one going into Solomon's Temple?" inquired a worker.

"It sure is!" replied the other.

"Right up front where everyone can see it, too!"

"Oh, no," cried the cedar brokenly. "Do not make an open shame of me, now that I have lost all my beauty that I once possessed!"

He closed his eyes and wept bitterly, but it was in vain. In a few days, when he was well dried, he was carried to the magnificent new Temple and placed upright as a prominent pillar in the building. Ashamed, he tried to hide its face in embarrassment and dismay. How could these people be so cruel as to make a public laughing stock of it!

Unhappily, it waited with sinking heart for the people to come by and make fun of its disgrace.

They did come by—but they did not laugh. With amazement, the cedar listened as he heard their loud exclamations.

"Such beauty!" they cried with reverence and awe. "How fitting to have this splendor in the Temple of God!"

Puzzled, the cedar ventured a look at them. With open mouths and shining eyes, they were admiring it and praising God. It simply did not understand. Quickly, it glanced down at itself and almost fell over with surprise.

From head to toe, it was clothed in radiant, shimmering pure gold, in which was reflected the joy and worship of the people. So *that* was the stuff which the workmen had plastered upon it so generously! Gratitude welled up in its heart with its new understanding. God had heard its prayer and had been preparing it for the place it had requested!

Humbly, the cedar squared its shoulders and lifted its

head, radiant inside and out.

"Surely the natural beauty that I possessed in the forest has disappeared, but I have been given a new splendor; moreover here in the Temple of the Lord I may surely serve God in a choice place, and inspire and bless the hearts of men as well! Fortunate indeed am I."

And the cedar's unpleasant experiences were remembered only as a stepping stone to a glorious place of holy service.

Adam, Eve, and the Snake

BY MENAHEM STERN

WHEN Adam and Eve were driven out of the Garden of Eden they found life very hard. They had to uproot trees in dense forests in order to farm the land or to graze their sheep and cattle on it. But above all they had to defend themselves against wild beasts which roamed the forests. No wonder that Adam and Eve were unhappy and restless, and found it difficult to stay in one place for a long time.

They wandered constantly, dreaming that they would find a place where life would be as pleasant and easy as in the Garden of Eden.

One day they came to a river abundant with fish and many fruit trees growing on its shores. As if to please their sense of beauty, majestic mountains rose on the river's opposite bank.

For once Adam and Eve were favorably impressed by the pleasant countryside and by the abundance of food.

Still, they reminded themselves of the wonders of the Garden of Eden which they had so foolishly lost. When this happened, they felt sad, but on second thought they decided

to settle in this lovely place and thus put an end to their wandering.

Meanwhile the snake, which had once slyly gotten Eve to eat the forbidden fruit, was lonely and glum in the Garden of Eden. One morning, as it stretched lazily in the sunlight, the snake was filled with self-pity.

"Because I am so clever," it thought, "I have nothing in common with any of the animals that live in the Garden of Eden. The only creatures whose company I found interesting were the two human beings who used to live here."

The snake felt a sudden stab of guilt.

"I feel sorry for Adam and Eve for losing the pleasant life they enjoyed here, although they have profited because they are now much wiser, for which they should of course thank me! But never mind. Let me see how the two human beings are making their way in the hard life outside the Garden of Eden." And the snake grinned in self-satisfaction as it slithered out of the Garden.

Illustrated by Bill Giacalone

When on one rainy afternoon, after a long journey, the snake came to the foot of a hill atop which stood the house of Adam and Eve, it blinked in bewilderment.

"What is this?" it gasped. For it had never before seen a *house*. Then the idea that life within this building must be pleasant because it was sheltered from cold and rain flashed through the mind of the reptile, and deep envy of Adam and Eve surged through the snake.

"I started off as the cleverest creature in the Garden. But now the human beings are far ahead of me," angrily thought the snake. At once all its friendly feelings towards Adam and Eve were forgotten. Jealousy quickly grew into savage hatred, and the snake started crawling up the hill with murder in its heart.

At this moment a huge dog, barking furiously, dashed out of the house.

The snake was ready to sink its poison fangs into the dog when Adam rushed to the rescue. The man looked big and strong, and the long heavy stick in his hand filled the snake with fear. After the snake had retreated from the hill it realized what a difference there was between man and itself. And it remembered the Lord's saying: "Human beings shall bruise your head and you shall bruise their heel."

And the snake slunk sadly away.

King Solomon and the Shamir

KING Solomon, the wisest man of men, resolved to build a Temple dedicated to the glory of the God of Israel. He remembered the sacred words of the Bible: "And if thou make Me an altar of stone, thou shalt not build it of hewn stones; for if thou lift up thy tool upon it, thou has made it unclean" (Exodus 20:22) . The tools of iron symbolized the sword, the instrument of war and death; so Solomon decided that in building the Temple no instrument of iron should be used.

But how could one split immense blocks of stone, or cut down huge trees, if the workmen were not allowed to use metal implements? In despair the king summoned the wisest men in his kingdom. After a while one of them arose and spoke:

"Long live the king! Among the countless creatures of the Most High there is one which can cut stone better than the sharpest tool of iron. It is called the Shamir, or diamond insect. Its size is that of a grain of barley. Yet it can split the hardest stone by merely touching it. And iron is broken by its mere presence."

There was joy in Solomon's heart. "Tell me," he asked, "Where is this marvelous little worm to be found?"

"Aren't you ruler of all the spirits and demons?" replied the counselor. "Seek their aid, and you will find the Shamir."

Solomon looked at the ring on his right hand and read the Holy Name of God engraved thereon.

At once a demon appeared before him and cried, "What is your wish, Solomon, King of Israel?"

"I command you," said Solomon, "to tell me where the worm Shamir is to be found."

In trembling voice the demon replied, "Mighty king of men and spirits! It is only Ashmodai our king who knows the secret."

"Tell me," interrupted King Solomon, "where does Ashmodai, the king of the demons, dwell?"

"Ashmodai's palace," said the demon, "is built on the top

of a very high mountain. There he has dug a deep well. Daily he fetches his drinking water from this well. He then closes up the mouth of the well with an enormous rock, which he seals with his signet ring. At sunset he returns to his home. He examines the seal, to see if it has been tampered with in his absence. He then uncovers the well and drinks of the water, and seals it afresh."

Solomon then summoned his brave captain and friend Benaiah, saying, "Go and capture Ashmodai, and bring him before me. To aid you, I give you this golden chain engraved with the Holy Name of God. Take with you also this large bundle of white wool and these skins full of strong wine."

After many days of hard riding across the great desert Benaiah finally reached his destination. Never had he seen such a deserted spot. But Benaiah feared neither man nor spirit, for on his finger he wore King Solomon's signet ring. He began to climb the mountain. Half way up, he bored a hole and found the well. He drew off the water and stuffed the hole with the wool he had brought with him. Near the hole, Benaiah made an opening into the well. Through it he poured all the wine in the skins. Then he concealed himself and waited for the arrival of the king of the demons.

Soon after sunset Ashmodai drew nigh. He examined the seal, rolled away the rock, and quenched his thirst. The fragrant wine overpowered him, and he felt drowsy. His head became heavy, his body staggered and his knees gave way. At last he fell to the ground and slept soundly.

Benaiah now threw the golden chain around Ashmodai's neck and sealed it with the golden signet ring engraved with the Divine Name.

When Ashmodai awoke he saw the golden chain around his neck. He groaned so loudly that the mountain shook.

It was no use. He could not rise. He looked at Benaiah and cried, "Is it you who has bewitched me?"

"Yes," replied Benaiah. "Come now. We will go at once to King Solomon, your master. Arise and follow me!"

When they arrived in Jerusalem, Benaiah conducted his captive to the royal presence.

Solomon said: "I merely demand one little service of you. I wish to build a great Temple to the glory of the Creator of heaven and earth, and for this purpose I require the services of the wonderful worm Shamir. Where can I find this tiny creature?"

"O wisest of mortals," replied Ashmodai, "don't you know that the Shamir has not been placed in my charge?"

"Where is it?" thundered Solomon. "Speak, slave! And speak truly."

"Mighty master," replied Ashmodai. "Since the days of Moses, who employed the Shamir when writing on the stone tablets of the Law, the worm has been entrusted to the care of the Prince of the Sea, who has given it into the charge of the wild thrush. The thrush lives in a nest built on the top of a very high mountain. Whenever he goes from his nest he takes the Shamir with him, carrying it beneath his wing."

Once again King Solomon summoned Benaiah, and sent him to bring the Shamir back to the Holy City.

"Take with you," said the king, "a glass cover, a little wool and a small leaden box."

Benaiah set out on his journey, crossing hill and dale, stream and desert. At last he discovered the nest of the wild thrush. In the nest were only tiny fledglings. Benaiah covered the nest with the glass. He then hid and waited.

When the thrush returned, the glass prevented him from entering the nest. He saw his helpless young, and flapped his wings and screeched loudly. But he could not break the glass. The young birds, frightened by the noise, also began to screech.

Again and again he tried to smash the glass. Finally, he decided to make use of the precious treasure entrusted to his care. He took the Shamir from beneath his wing and put it on the glass. Lo, the glass split into pieces as soon as it was touched by the wonderful worm. At that instant Benaiah raised a lusty cry and frightened the thrush so that he dropped the Shamir. It had barely touched the ground when Benaiah seized it and carefully placed it in the wool and put the tiny bundle into the small leaden box which he had brought at Solomon's command.

Without lingering a moment, Benaiah set out on his homeward journey, rejoicing greatly at his success. Benaiah reached Jerusalem in safety and delivered to King Solomon the wonderful worm. With its help the wise king built the Temple; but thereafter the Shamir disappeared, and to this very day no one knows where it is to be found.

The Feverfew

BY BARUCH CIZIK

IN THE time of Pharaoh, king of Egypt, the children of Israel labored with mortar and with bricks and they built cities for Pharaoh, the cities of Pithom and Raamses. And Pharaoh commanded all his people, saying, "Every son that is born to the Israelites you shall cast into the Nile and every daughter you shall save alive." But the Jewish mothers sought for ways to hide their baby sons from Pharaoh's wicked guards, and they concealed them in the bushes and trees on the banks of the Nile. Thus the Jewish children grew up in the heart of nature, and they made friends with the cattle of the field and the beasts of the land, and became as fleet-footed as the deer and spry as the birds.

At sunrise when the bulbul-bird and his mate awoke from their sleep and burst into song in notes thin and clear as a flute's, the children joined in the singing, and when they heard the summons of the warbler, they rose and went forth to gather herbs and mushrooms.

When the day was ended and darkness fell and the quivering wail of the jackal was heard, the little ones climbed up to beds their mothers had made for them in the branches of the trees. Thus the children grew, safe and sound in the arms of nature. And if one of them fell ill, they knew the plants that might be used as remedies. Their favorite was the whitecrowned feverfew: by sucking its tiny leaves, they were safe from the dreaded malaria.

And it came to pass that Pharaoh, king of Egypt, fell ill, and he sought advice from his magicians. And the magicians commanded that some of the feverfew flowers that grew on the banks of the Nile should be brought to them, that they might be boiled in water and their juice served to the suffering king.

So Pharaoh sent his attendants to gather some of these flowers. And as they were plucking them, they drew nearer and nearer to the hiding-place of the Jewish children. But the children's friends, the sharp-eared birds, flew from bough to bough, chirping all the while, to warn the children of the danger hovering over them. And the feverfew flowers, trembling with fear, shed the petals of their white crowns so that only their hearts, their golden hearts, remained.

The children of the Israelites heeded the warning of the birds and the flowers. Quickly they climbed up into their hiding-places among the branches. There they sat in silence and together with the birds listened intently to every sound about them.

When the king's attendants, having searched very carefully, saw that there were no flowers there about with white crowns such as the magicians had described to them, they turned away and went to look for them elsewhere.

Thus it was that the Jewish children escaped from the cruel king who had sought to do away with them.

And when these children grew up and together with their

Illustrated by Lili Cassel Wronker

fathers and mothers left the land of Egypt they remembered with deep gratitude the golden-hearted feverfew and took a great many of these flowers with them.

Since that time these flowers with their golden hearts but bereft of their white crowns grow all over the desert and all over the land of Israel, for they were sown in great abundance by the Israelites when they came forth out of Egypt.

A Legend of the Red Sea

BY MENAHEM STERN

WHEN the news reached the king of the Red Sea that the Egyptians were pursuing the Israelites, he rose from his coral throne and said to the waters:

"Moses has freed the children of Israel. But Pharaoh hopes to drive the Israelites into the sea. To save themselves, the Israelites must cross our waters.

"Now hear my instructions, waters! Make a path, so that Moses and his people will be able to reach the shore safely."

Most of the waters were in favor of helping the children of Israel. They bubbled happily and cried in excitement:

"We waters love freedom and endless space, so we know what freedom means to Hebrews. We will gladly fulfill your wish, O king."

But some of the waters opposed the king's orders. They foamed angrily and roared:

"Why should we be good to human beings? They don't care about us! Let them build boats and sail to safety in *them* if they can!"

The obedient, helpful waters spoke patiently and wisely:

"Don't you know what happened in Egypt? Because Pharaoh was so stubborn and wicked, God turned all the waters in Egypt to blood. Would you want the same fate to happen to us?"

The uncooperative waters grew even angrier at this.

"The sea is for fish and pearls, and not for human beings. We shall never allow ourselves to be parted just so that people may walk through us!"

But the good waters refused to give up. Their waves lapped quietly as they used every means of persuasion. They said:

"Our distant relative, the River Nile, once carried a basket in which lay the baby Moses. Now Moses the Liberator and his people have come to our shore. Will we suddenly become merciless? Shall we not divide and make a way until all the men, women, and children have reached safety?"

The bad waters did not know how to answer, so they contented themselves by swelling up, roaring fiercely, and slapping their wild waves against the peace-loving waters.

The Red Sea became very stormy. The old king of the Red Sea rushed to the surface. With watery eyes he wept as he threw himself against the seashore and saw multitudes of fearful, desperate Hebrews, and far behind them, in a cloud of dust, Pharaoh's war chariots rushing madly towards their prey.

At this moment Moses, leader of his people, stepped out from the great throng of Israelites and lifted his staff. A historic event was to take place.

"Some of my waters are merciless and disobedient. I must help the childen of Israel or they will perish!" thought the old king of the Red Sea. And he called for the mightiest winds to help him divide the sea.

The winds swooped down upon the waters.

"I brought the locusts upon the Egyptian fields and gar-

dens and I am now ready to help the Israelites against their enemies!" screamed one wind.

"And I," roared another wind, "I drove the hail clouds over the towns and villages of Egypt."

Now both winds lashed the bad waters with all their fury. And lo, the wicked waters were parted from the good waters, so that the Red Sea split widely, and a path was opened in the heart of the sea.

And as Moses and the children of Israel trod the dry path that led them to safety, the old king of the Red Sea sat on his coral throne and a smile of happiness played on his face.

Illustrated by E. Schloss

Cupbearer to the King

BY LEON SPITZ

DAVID was proud of his father, Nehemiah, the sage who was cupbearer to the Persian King Artaxerxes at the palace in Shushan. But David's mother had died, and David and his father grieved for her. When David was chosen by Asphenaz, chief of the king's magicians, to be one of the king's wards, his father looked into his sparkling black eyes, and stroked his dark curly hair. "Even in the royal palace, I charge you, my son," he said, "to uphold the honor of our people and remain steadfast to the laws of Moses."

Three years passed, and David—now fifteen years old—returned to his father's house, a tall youth, strong in body, with bronzed face and a ready smile.

One night their kinsman Hanai arrived from the land of Judea, and he spoke to them about Jerusalem, which was far away, and about the Jews who had some years ago returned there from Persia.

"The walls of Jerusalem are broken down and the gates are burned with fire," Hanai said sadly, "so that our people are harassed by Arabians and the Horonites and the Ammonites."

When they heard these words, David and his father were saddened, and they prayed for the peace of Jerusalem.

David was not satisfied with prayer. "Father," he called out, "our people need us in Jerusalem. Let another man serve the king his cup of wine."

His father was aroused by his son's enthusiasm. "Yes," he said. "David, you and I shall bathe and anoint ourselves with myrrh, put on garments of velvet, and bind on our heads turbans of purple trimmed with silver cord, as befits those who appear in the presence of the king."

As they entered the king's vast throne-room, David looked about him with great curiosity. The hangings on the walls were of white, fine linen bordered with cords of purple. A large variety of silver lamps were suspended from the high, vauited ceiling. The floor was paved with tiles of green and white marble.

The king and his fair queen sat in their gold and velvet robes on massive thrones of ivory. Behind them and over them towered the colossal idol of Baal, the mighty god of ancient Babylon.

Nehemiah bowed before the king and pleaded, "Will the king of kings permit his servant to speak?"

"You have my leave," said Artaxerxes graciously.

Nehemiah spoke: "Grief lodges in my heart for the reason that the city of my fathers lies waste and the gates thereof are consumed with fire."

"What do you request of me?" the king demanded.

Nehemiah said boldly, "If it please my lord the king, send me to Jerusalem, the city of my fathers, that I may rebuild it."

David dared not speak, but in his heart he prayed ardently that Artaxerxes should grant his father's petition.

At last the king spoke. "I shall command my scribe to bestow upon you a scroll proclaiming that I have this day appointed you governor of Jerusalem."

Joy surged into David's soul. Then his father took him by the hand and they departed from the king's presence.

Nehemiah commanded the servants of his household to load the pack-camels with provisions for the long journey across the wilderness. A huge chest filled with golden shekels he strapped to his camel's back. Before he mounted his own handsome animal, David stuck a shofar into his girdle, for he excelled in blowing the ram's horn and took pride in

his skill.

The journey was long. Again their caravan was forced to engage in brisk skirmishes with wild bands of raiders who pounced upon them from ambushes; but when the raiders

Illustrated by Cyla London

saw that Nehemiah's caravan was strongly protected, they wheeled their camels about and vanished quickly from sight.

At last the wretchedly battered walls of Jerusalem loomed against the purple sunset. What a sorry sight they made!

The once towering ramparts were crumbling. The gates were gaping, burnt out breaches. No watchman was any-where about, so the caravan trudged toward the city and pitched tents in a half-deserted spot near the entrance.

After they had rested a short while, Nehemiah summoned two of his servants. "We ride this night to inspect the walls of the city."

"Take me with you, father," David begged.

Nehemiah gave his approval and David rode out with them. The road was narrow, and in the dark was well nigh impassable. So after a while they dismounted and continued on foot. They walked over to the fountain-gate and then to the king's pool. They passed the broken inner gates, and then tarried to drink from the Dragon's Well. And every-where they beheld ruin and destruction. When they return-ed to their caravan, David lay down to sleep on a rug in the tent by his father's side—sad of heart.

*   *   *

The arrival of the caravan caused a stir among the people of Jerusalem. Groups of men, among whom were hewers of wood, and artisans who worked with brass and copper, and bakers, and sellers of oil and of soap, came to look. Together with their wives and little children they stood about and stared at the newcomers.

One portly, pleasant-faced man pushed his way through the crowd and asked Nehemiah, "Who are you? and whence do you come?"

"We have come from royal Shushan, the capital city of Persia," Nehemiah replied. "I wish to speak to the elders and the priests of Jerusalem."

The man regarded Nehemiah long and searchingly and, said, "My name is Shallum, of the house of Judah, and I am the ruler of this district of the city. I shall guide you to Eliashib, the chamberlain of the Temple."

"But first my son and I shall visit the Temple and offer prayer to thank the Lord for our safe journey," Nehemiah said.

Shallum led them to the little sanctuary which stood next to the house of the chamberlain. The sanctuary was furnished simply. David gazed with reverence at the holy ark, the golden menorah, the altar of sacrifice. And he knelt by his father's side in prayer. . . .

Then they arose and followed Shallum to the house of Eliashib. The host, black-bearded and wearing a Kohen's robes and the velvet ephod, greeted them with many smiles and bows, and ordered his servants to set before them a meal of dates, curdled cheese, barley-cake and goat's milk. Presently one after another the elders of Jerusalem and the priests of the Levite families assembled.

When they heard that Nehemiah was the *Tirshasha*—the governor sent to rule in Jerusalem in the name of the king— and that it was in his heart to rebuild the city and repair its walls, they greeted him with joy.

Yet one Shemiah, the son of Deliah, said in a complaining voice, "The people are too poor to support the household of a Tirshasha."

"Be assured," Nehemiah replied, "that I and my household, one hundred and twenty in number, will not demand the king's taxes, and I shall purchase with my own money the food we shall eat."

As the door now opened wide all stood up in respect for the aged man who entered.

"Greetings, Ezra!" they called out.

So this was the great Ezra, David said to himself—Ezra the Scribe, whom King Artaxerxes himself held in such esteem. The newcomer was indeed a venerable but also feeble man; his beard was snowy white and his eyes were pale, almost sightless. When he was told of Nehemiah's mission in Jerusalem, he embraced him and said in a quavering voice, *"Barukh ha-ba.* May the Lord prosper your errand, Nehemiah. And may the Lord bless you, too, my child," he continued, laying his hand on David's head

When the greetings were over, Nehemiah said to the elders, "Who will assist in repairing the walls of Jerusalem?'

Many answered, "Assign to each of us a district where we may build and repair the breaches in the wall."

And thus the work of repairing the walls of Jerusalem was begun.

Just one week later a band of riders, armed with long iron-tipped spears, carrying shields of thick leather, and mounted on powerful white mules, appeared at the city's gate near the King's Pool. David stood at his father's side and with them was Shallum, the elder of the house of Judah.

"Who are these men?" Nehemiah demanded.

"They are," said Shallum, "Sanballat the Horonite, and Geshem the Arabian, and Tobiah the Ammonite, he who took in marriage the sister of Eliashib."

"The Temple chamberlain's sister wedded to an Ammonite?" Nehemiah cried out.

"This Eliashib will need watching," David said to himself.

"These men intend us evil," Nehemiah resumed. "Nevertheless, as the king's governor, I shall greet them and tell

them of my mission."

By this time the three foremost riders had dismounted and approached. All three of them were sturdily built and thick-bearded, and all were richly dressed. From the side of each dangled a heavy silver-hilted sword.

"Are you he who pretends to be the Tirshasha?" Tobiah arrogantly demanded.

"I *am* the Tirshasha," Nehemiah said sternly.

The Arabian in his turn spoke up with a sneer. "Is it with this rabble that you will rebuild Jerusalem? Will they revive the stones out of the heaps of rubbish? If a fox went up, he shall break down your walls."

"The Lord will gird us with strength," Nehemiah said confidently.

Sanballat the Horonite now burnt with wrath. "Be warned!" he blustered. "We are tribal chiefs. My armed men and the armed men of these chiefs will sweep your servants away and scatter them as the wind scatters the chaff."

"Will you resist the authority of King Artaxerxes?" Nehemiah challenged Sanballat.

The Horonite laughed scornfully. "The king of kings is far away, very far away."

"And you are a lying pretender," the Ammonite broke in snorting.

"You dare insult my honored father!" David cried out, and made to leap at the Ammonite.

"No, no, my son," Nehemiah restrained him. "The king's scroll will prove without question that I am in truth the Tirshasha." From under his robe he drew out the scroll and showed it to the others.

For a moment the others were taken aback. Sanballat was the first to recover. "You forged the scroll," he jeered.

Before Nehemiah could deny the foul accusation, the three chieftains turned their mules about and galloped off, followed by their henchmen, at a breakneck speed.

* * *

As the Jews of Jerusalem went on with the labor of repairing the city's walls, Nehemiah commanded the servants of his household, "You shall at no time let go of your spears and your shields and your bows. The half of you," he went on, "shall guard during the night against the menace of the marauders. The work is large and we are separated on the wall, one far from another. Therefore, it shall be that in whatever place you may hear the sound of the shofar, you shall all rush to that place."

"I shall blow the shofar mightily," David said.

One night as David walked through a dark alley on his way to his father's house, two ruffians pounced on him, and one muttered gruffly, "If you value your life, do not cry out."

Summoning all his courage, David demanded, "What do you want with me?"

The second attacker said, "Inform your father that should he remain in Jerusalem, you, his son, will be captured and slain."

Having made their threat, the two ruffians let go of David and disappeared into the night.

At first David wanted to follow them, but after a moment he wisely decided to report the matter to the Tirshasha.

"Our enemies are evil men," Nehemiah said, "and they are determined to compel me to leave Jerusalem."

"Jerusalem needs you," David protested. "You must stay here."

"Yes, I must stay here," Nehemiah replied. "But I'll send you back to Shushan, where the hands of my enemies cannot reach out to you to do you harm."

"I'll not leave you, Father," David cried out hotly. "Here we both stay and together we'll defy our enemies."

On the following day, towards noon, as David passed the house of Nehemiah, the man's wife, the Lady Noadiah, stopped him.

"Drink," she said cordially; "here is honeyed wine which I have cooled."

Gratefully, David sipped the cooling drink.

"All Jerusalem," the woman continued, "holds your father, the Tirshasha, in great esteem. But he looks so pale and wan from overwork. Give him this bottle of the wine of raisins in which I mixed a healing balm. Let him drink it tonight that his strength be restored in the morning."

David took the wine-jug from the woman's hands and strode off.

"I have heard it said," he told his father, "that the woman is a healer."

Nehemiah smiled. "I shall drink the wine before I lie down to rest tonight."

It was still an hour before bedtime, so David went out into the street for a stroll. As he neared the house of Eliashib, he caught sight of a woman approaching. Her furtive movements aroused his suspicion. As she pushed away the shawl from her face, David recognized her. "The Lady Noadiah!" he cried out, startled. "She visits the house of the Temple chamberlain alone and stealthily . . . And she gave me wine for the Tirshasha to drink." There was something foul afoot, he decided. He must not lose a moment in warning his father. Hastily he retracted his steps to his father's house and rushed into Nehemiah's presence.

"Father," he cried breathlessly, "don't drink the wine I brought you!"

"But you, yourself, fetched it to me," Nehemiah said.

"Only a few moments ago," David explained, "I saw the Lady Noadiah enter the chamberlain's house alone and veiled! She looked suspicious to me!"

Nehemiah nodded. "Eliashib the Temple chamberlain," he said, "is a kinsman of the Ammonite lord. And this woman gave you a draught for me to drink."

"But why?" David asked. "Why did Lady Noadiah give me wine for you to drink?"

"It may well be," his father said, "that they are plotting with the Ammonites to attack Jerusalem this very night. Perhaps they mixed a sleeping potion into the drink so that I would fall into a heavy slumber while they attacked. They intend that our people should lose faith in me . . . My son, I shall not drink the wine. And this night I shall sleep in the open on the city wall."

"I too shall keep watch," David said. "And I'll keep my shofar in my belt."

The night was overcast with thick clouds. The hours dragged slowly. David forced himself to keep his eyes from closing. Then as midnight struck, the sounds of the heavy tramping of armed beasts reached him. Instantly David put his shofar to his lips and sounded a loud long blast. At his side his father leaped up with a start. Armed men stirred briskly, shook the sleep out of their eyes, and took up their stations on the battlement. David repeated his shofar blasts again and again, and more and more armed men came running to the spot from different directions.

The advance of the mules and their riders came to a standstill.

Sanballat stood up in his stirrups scowling fiercely. "We have been discovered," he spat out. "Let's ride back."

But Tobiah called out, "Hold for a moment . . ."

His powerful voice thundered in the night. "Hear me, Nehemiah! You have set yourself up as a ruler in Jerusalem. You plot rebellion again Artaxerxes, the king of kings. Tattenai, the king's governor beyond the Jordan, shall hear of this."

The troop rode off.

"What will happen now?" David asked anxiously. "Will the king's governor heed their false accusations?"

Nehemiah turned to Shallum. "What do you think?"

Shallum said, "Tattenai, the king's governor beyond the Jordan, is reputed to be a greedy man, and I fear he will welcome their gifts of gold."

Nehemiah said firmly, "I shall go on repairing the walls of Jerusalem."

And David's eyes shone with pride at his father's courage.

* * *

Shallum sighed. "It's a wonder to me," said he, "that Tattenai the governor has not ordered you to desist from the work before this."

"This can only mean one thing," Nehemiah said. "Tattenai has gone forth to carry the false accusation against me to the king. I must go to Shushan at once to answer his charges."

"You will desert us here in Jerusalem!" Shallum protested. "What if the people should think that you have left us in fear of Tattenai, never to return?"

"I shall return," Nehemiah said sternly.

But Shallum did not yield. "The journey will take many months," he said. "In the meantime the traitors within the city will join hands with the enemies outside. Only you, Nehemiah, can prevail against them. You must not leave us."

"But should Tattenai accuse me in the presence of King Artaxerxes," Nehemiah persisted, "who will be there to defend me?"

David's eyes lit up. "I'll defend you," he called out.

"You?" His father regarded him uncertainly. "Only a fortnight ago I wished to send you to Shushan and you refused to go."

David grinned. "You wished me to flee our enemies"
"And now?"

"Now I would go to Shushan to face our enemies and do
battle with them."

Nehemiah hesitated . . . But David ran on eagerly. "You
know I was a ward of the king and I know the ways of the
palace. I'll foil their plot!"

Nehemiah embraced David. "My son," he said, "you shall
leave this night before the Ammonite learns of your
errand."

Within the hour David had received the blessing of Ezra
and had left the city escorted by two trusted men on the
fleetest camels Nehemiah was able to procure. All through
that first night they rode, and in the heat of the following
day, until they arrived at the banks of the Jordan. On the
second night they slept in a clump of thick bushes, and at
dawn they rode forth again.

"We should be safe now," one of David's companions
said. "If the Ammonite hasn't caught up with us by now, it
is a sure sign that he has not learned of our departure."

"We must continue to be wary," said David. "They have
fleet horses and we have not yet ridden far."

Hardly had David finished speaking when a great cloud
of dust signaled the approach of Tobiah, the Ammonite,
with ten of his men.

David braced himself for a desperate fight. But how could
he face eleven men? Suddenly he smiled.

"We shall charge the Ammonites with the speed of the
wind," he called blithely to his two companions. "And as
we ride, let us shout with all our strength, "For the Lord
and for Nehemiah!"

"But Nehemiah isn't with us!" said o n e of his companions.

"Our battle-cry will fool them into thinking that Nehemiah himself follows us with a whole troop."

So they charged, shouting, "For the L o r d and Nehemiah!"

David's ruse worked. "Nehemiah! Nehemiah himself is pursuing us!" screamed Tobiah's men. In a moment they had fled in confusion.

"Thank the Lord our trick succeeded," David exulted. "Now we ride on unhindered to Shushan!"

At last David reached Shushan and obtained an audience with the king. When David entered the throne room he saw that Tattenai, the king's wily governor, had the ear of Artaxerxes. Nehemiah, Tattenai was saying, had brought unrest into a country where peace had ruled. Moreover, said Tattenai, despite the great honors Artaxerxes had bestowed upon him, Nehemiah was secretly plotting to proclaim himself king of Jerusalem. Nehemiah deserved to die a rogue's death—on the gallows.

The king's wrath burnt fiercely. Despair gripped David. He knew he could not simply shout that Tattenai was a liar and a traitor. He must handle the matter more carefully.

"My lord king," he pleaded, "may a son speak in defense of his father?"

"Who are you, lad?" the king demanded.

"I am the son of Nehemiah," said David.

The king hesitated . . . He was still under the spell of Tattenai's false charges. And he remained suddenly silent.

Now the queen intervened. "Surely," she said, "my lord will hearken to the youth."

The king hesitated, but only for a moment. "It shall not be said," he declared, "that King Artaxerxes denies justice to anyone." He nodded to David to proceed.

"My lord king," David spoke up. "Tattenai the governor made grave charges against my honored father. But has he brought forward any proof that he spoke truth? . . . The Ammonite, the Moabite, the Edomite lords—jealous of the honor which King Artaxerxes bestowed upon him—have sought to intimidate him. The lords even threatened to slay me, Nehemiah's son, when my father refused to abandon the task with which you entrusted him."

"My lord king," Tattenai blurted out, "the lad babbles meaningless nonsense."

But David continued: "These many years Nehemiah, my father and your servant, has served you, King Artaxerxes, faithfully and with devotion."

"That is so," Artaxerxes grudgingly admitted.

David went on: "I brought with me a scroll from Ezra the Sage, esteemed by the king for his piety and goodness. Will the king command one of the royal scribes to read it aloud?"

"The scroll shall be read."

The scribe unrolled the scroll and read: "Ezra, the Scribe, to Artaxerxes, king of kings, greetings! David, the son of Nehemiah, is a goodly lad and he speaketh words of truth and honor."

The king's eyes softened. "Where did you obtain this scroll?" he asked.

"I received it from the hands of Ezra himself," David said.

"Is Ezra still alive?" Artaxerxes asked.

"The great Ezra is alive in Jerusalem and he aids my father, Nehemiah, in carrying out the orders of the king of kings."

David rejoiced to see Artaxerxes grow mellow, and he decided to take a step which might mean his very life.

"My lord king," he called out, "if Nehemiah plotted treason, would he send me, his only son, to the king's palace as a hostage?"

Artaxerxes stiffened. "And you love your father so well," he said, "that you have come of your own free will to be a hostage for him?"

"Yes, O king of kings." David bowed low.

"Arise, son of Nehemiah," Artaxerxes said, "and hear my decree. You will return to your father. Say to Nehemiah: 'Thus said Artaxerxes: My servant, Nehemiah, shall ever enjoy the king's favor'."

David clapped his hands in joy. He rose and departed, the happiest youth in all the land.

When on the fourteenth day of the seventh month, which is the month of Tishri, David reappeared in Jerusalem, he exulted at the sight of the walls of his beloved city standing up strong and nobly.

It was the eve of the Feast of Sukkot, so that the people assembled into Jerusalem from all parts of the land and marched in a procession carrying palm branches and golden-yellow citrons unto the sanctuary of the Lord. Old Ezra, the priestly scribe, poured an offering of pure oil on the altar and blessed the city which Nehemiah had fortified.

There was great gladness in Jerusalem.

And David, the son of Nehemiah, the king's cupbearer, sounded his shofar—blast after blast, exultant, triumphant blasts.

Joshua and the Sun

BY MENAHEM STERN

AFTER THE DEATH of Moses, Joshua became the leader of the children of Israel. He led our people into the Promised Land. But there were enemies who resisted the march of the Israelites. Joshua waged many battles against the foe, and little by little the land of Canaan became the land of Israel. One town after another fell to the victorious Joshua and his brave men.

One day the sun, beaming down on the plains of Jordan, beheld the tribe known as the Amorites fleeing before the Israelites in great confusion. The sun grew fearful of Joshua, and said to itself:

"Those Amorites are my faithful followers. They worship me! I am their god. They sing my praises morning and night. Now they are being wiped out by the Israelites. Soon the children of Israel will occupy the whole land and there will be no one left to bow down and pray to me!"

A cloud darkened the face of the sun. "These Hebrews!" it mused. "They have wandered for many years in the wilderness. They're nomads, that's all. They don't know how to appreciate my beauty, nor are they thankful for the great good I do in the world. Instead of revering me, they bow

and pray to a God of Justice and Righteousness who can't even be seen or heard.

"I shall take away my light from Joshua and the children of Israel so that they will not see how to conquer my devoted worshippers. Though it is the middle of the day, I will set! The Israelites will have to fight in the darkness. Ha! Joshua and his warriors fight well enough when I generously give my light, but they will not do half as well in the darkness. Let them lose the battle!"

And the sun suddenly began to slip into the West. As it set, a pale moon appeared over the plains of Jordan.

Illustrated by Bill Giacalone

Now a fear overwhelmed the Israelites. Never had they seen such a strange sight. The advance guard broke ranks and retreated in haste. The Amorites, on the other hand, greeted the sun's setting with shouts of gratitude and joy. They thought the sun-god was coming to their aid. This would turn the tide of battle against the Israelites, they thought. So they rushed courageously into the attack.

But Joshua refused to yield so easily. "There is something odd about the sun today," he said "It goes down too soon and too speedily. I sense danger. I'd better stop the sun right now!"

Then, standing on top of a hill and watching the sun's westward progress with worried eyes, Joshua remembered the promise which God had given. The children of Israel *would inherit Canaan,* He had said. Whereupon Joshua took fresh courage, and in a clear, steady voice filled with confidence and faith, he exclaimed: "Sun, stand still upon Gibeon; and you, Moon, in the valley of Aijalon!"

No sooner had the words come out of Joshua's mouth than the sun trembled and stood still in its place.

Ashamed and helpless, the sun thought: "I am not as powerful as I thought I was. The God of the children of Israel and of all human beings, is also the master over light and darkness. The truth is that He is also *my* God and I am only a small part of His creation. It must be the will of God that the Israelites win the war and inherit the Promised Land."

So the sun chased away all the clouds and shone on the plains of Jordan until Joshua and his people had conquered the Amorites. When the battle was over and the Israelites were weary but victorious, the sun went down.

In Naboth's Vineyard

BY MENAHEM STERN

KING AHAB and Queen Jezebel were wicked rulers, as the Bible tells us. One day the country was stirred by the cruel death of a farmer named Naboth, whose vineyard had been seized by the royal couple.

When the sad news reached the vineyard, the trees felt sorrow and anger. In the strong wind, many voices of protest were heard.

"Naboth was murdered! Our rightful and devoted owner!" exclaimed a blooming grapevine as in grief it drooped its clusters of grapes.

A vine near the outer fence moaned: "In the heat of the day he watered us and in the cool nights he protected our grapes from foxes and thieves."

In another part of the vineyard a vine shook its branches angrily and said:

"Honest Naboth was stoned by order of the king and queen!"

Then all the vines grew quiet as the eldest among them spoke:

"King Ahab and Queen Jezebel now own the vineyard. Soon the king's servants will come to pick our grapes. Over the wine made from our fruit blessings will be chanted to idols instead of to the God of Israel and of the whole world. Brothers and sisters! Let us all shed our fruit so that it may not fall into the royal pickers' hands!"

"You are right!" replied the vines. And they rustled restlessly in the growing wind until their grapes had fallen to the ground.

One exception was a young vine that grew in a sheltered corner of the arbor. Gaily he said:

"All my life I dreamed of the day when from my grapes wine would be pressed to be served in the royal palace. Now my dream will come true."

How disappointed were Ahab's servants when they came to pick the grapes, for all they saw were empty vines. Then they beheld the young vine which still bore fruit. Eagerly they started to pick the grapes.

Suddenly, from the valley of the Jordan a flock of ravens appeared. These were no ordinary birds. They were the very ravens which, at God's command, had fed the Prophet Elijah with flesh and bread when he was a fugitive.

To the amazement of the royal servants, they swooped down upon the solitary vine, covering it with their flapping black wings. In a moment they had eaten all the grapes. Then they flew away, leaving a mourning vineyard and a royal couple whose punishment for evil deeds had now begun.

Illustrated by E. Schloss

The Walls of Jericho

MOSES was dead! The mighty prophet who had brought the children of Israel to the very threshold of the Promised Land was gone. The people were on edge. Could Joshua really take his place?

Fragments of heated conversation drifted through the closed flap of Joshua's tent, where he pored over battle plans. With deft fingers he flipped through diagrammed leaves of parchment.

Outside, voices became louder and intruded upon Joshua's thoughts.

"I tell you," a sharp voice stated, "without Moses, Joshua is as helpless as any of us!"

"He brought us all safely over the swollen floodtides of the Jordan River," argued a second.

"A far cry from conquering Canaan," the former said in contempt. "Perhaps you all forget how headstrong Joshua has proven to be in times past. Moses had to scold him more than once."

"Yet Moses laid his hands on Joshua and gave him some of his own wisdom," quietly remarked a defender.

"As he did to seventy of the elders!" was the crisp reply.

At that point, a new challenger was heard, bringing a smile of recognition to Joshua's pained expression. Caleb had entered the picture. In his imagination, Joshua could see him moving in, stately and upright, fairly bristling with outraged indignation, his deep-set eagle eyes darting fiercely from one opponent to another.

"Now will you argue with Moses, or will it be with the Almighty?" The tones of the veteran fighter dripped with sarcasm. After all, they had both appointed Joshua to be their new captain!

In the silence that ensued the tent flap was lifted, and the angry Caleb entered unannounced.

"Welcome, friend Caleb," said Joshua warmly. "What would I do without you to come to my rescue?'

"Fresh young upstarts!" hissed Caleb in disgust.

Joshua noted that Caleb was still visibly disturbed.

"What will you do about Jericho?" inquired the warrior anxiously. "Jericho will not be easy to defeat."

Joshua nodded his head. "As a matter of fact, instructions have already been given to the people. A reaction may follow at any minute."

A commotion was heard in the camp. The low buzzing of aroused men rose to a rumble, accompanied by hurrying footsteps approaching the tent.

Without a word, Joshua rose to his feet and stepped outside, followed closely by Caleb.

"Let one of you speak at a time," said Joshua.

Each looked uncertainly at the other but after a moment of silence, a burly, black-eyed man pushed his way through the crowd and addressed Joshua.

"Sir," he said with scarcely concealed excitement, "we were willing to follow you as we did Moses until we heard of this ridiculous plan of attack. It is foolish to think we could overcome a strong, fortified city simply by marching around the walls and blowing trumpets. We are not madmen, nor do we wish to expose ourselves to needless danger and thus risk making helpless widows and orphans of our loved ones. Give us at least some reasonable hope of success."

As he stepped back into the group, a murmur of approval swelled among the rest of the men. Again Joshua raised his arm and quiet was restored. Fire seemed to flash from his brilliant blue eyes as Joshua scanned the faces before him.

When he spoke at last, the words fell like meteors among them.

"Even as the Almighty was with Moses, so has He promised to be with me. You will either believe this or choose another leader. Make your decision."

Slowly, one by one, they turned and went away. Only one elder waited, gave Joshua a pleading look, and simply said, "We have no choice." Then he, too, left.

"What is this?" queried Caleb in alarm. "What is your plan concerning this offensive?"

Briefly, Joshua outlined his instructions from the Lord.

"We are to march around the walls of Jericho once each day for six days. Seven priests will bear and blow trumpets of rams' horns, going before the Ark of the Covenant. No other sound is to be made. On the seventh day, we march seven times and then all the people will shout with a loud voice as the trumpets blow. So shall we take the city."

Caleb shook his head doubtfully.

"I trust you know the voice of the Lord, Joshua," he said sadly. "Otherwise, all will be lost."

Joshua gazed steadily into the sharp eyes of his friend. Reassured, Caleb gripped his hand and departed. Entering his tent, Joshua paced back and forth, mulling over the unpleasant discussion. His heart was sore within him. Doubt began to seep in. Suppose he had dreamed up a wild scheme and imagined it was God. He well knew the truth of Caleb's parting remark. Faster and faster beat his heart until he felt it would burst within him. He could not afford to make a mistake now.

Quickly he threw his cloak about him, hurried unseen from the tent and from the camp, and began to make his way toward Jericho. The miles disappeared swiftly under his rapid pace and he hardly noticed the sinking of the even-

ing sun. When at last he stood on the mountaintop over-looking the city, night had settled about him and the stars were glimmering above. With panting breath, he drew the light, dry air into his lungs. Below lay Jericho, dark and still, the high, massive walls silhouetted against the skyline. Surely this sealed fortress would take much battering and hammering. How had he ever thought a march and a shout could get the job done? He would go back to camp, confess his folly, and fall upon the mercy of the people.

While these conscience-stricken thoughts flooded his soul, the words of the Lord suddenly burned into his mind even as the words of the Law written upon the tablets of stone. "As I was with Moses, so I will be with thee: I will not fail thee, nor forsake thee."

Peace descended upon Joshua and he relaxed, inside and out. In that moment, he became aware of a figure standing beside him—a man with a drawn sword. Fearlessly he addressed the figure.

"Art thou for us, or for our enemies?"

The man answered, "Nay, but as captain of the host of

Illustrated by Bill Giacalone

the Lord am I now come."

Gratitude welled up in the heart of Joshua, and he worshiped the Lord with joy and confidence. Strengthened mightily in his own spirit, he retraced the long journey back to Gilgal and slipped into his tent and bed for a short nap before dawn.

The next day the march began. Once around the city, the trumpets blowing loudly, then back to camp; six days the pattern was repeated. On the seventh, the marching began at dawn and the city was circled seven times. At the completion, the priests gave a long blast with the rams' horns and Joshua ordered, "Shout; for the Lord has given you the city!" The silence of the lips of all the people was broken and they gave a great shout. Instantly the walls crumbled, and the shout of faith became a shout of victory as the forty thousand men of war swarmed in and took the city.

Moses indeed was dead, but now the people knew that the wisdom of Moses rested upon Joshua.

The Broken Tablets

BY MENAHEM STERN

AFTER MOSES had broken the Tablets bearing the Ten Commandments, the shattered pieces of stone complained bitterly to God.

"Lord of the Universe!" they said. "For long centuries did we await the coming of Moses. We did not mind the howling winds, nor the stabbing lightning, nor the scorching sun, for we cherished a great dream. Do we now deserve this harsh punishment? Is it our fault that during the time when Moses was on Mount Sinai some of the Israelites made

a golden calf and worshiped it?"

Silence swept the sandy plain, the long rows of Israelite tents, and towering Mount Sinai. Then the voice of God was heard:

"O fragments of stone, you are dearer to me than ever before, for it was not your sin that caused you to be broken. And because you were faithful, I promise that one day you will have an important task to fulfill."

A strong wind began to blow. It picked up the stone fragments and carried them towards Jerusalem, which was then a Jebusite town in Canaan. And all the pieces of stone, except one with very sharp edges, dropped on a mountain named Moriah, in the heart of Jerusalem.

The sharp-edged fragment was borne westward by the wind to the valley of Elah.

Years and generations and centuries passed. Then, one day, a brave shepherd boy named David picked up a sharp piece of stone, put it in his sling, and with all his strength

Illustrated by Uri Shulevitz

aimed it at the Philistine giant Goliath, who had mockingly challenged the Israelites.

"I must hit Goliath and save the Hebrews!" whispered the fragment, for it was indeed the keen-edged piece of the broken tablets. And it sped through the air and sank into the giant's forehead.

That day our people won a great victory and a stalwart shepherd began his rise to greatness and fame.

A quite different fate awaited the fragments on Mount Moriah. For a long time they unhappily watched the pagan idol-worship of the Jebusites. When David occupied the city and turned it into the capital of Israel, they were happy.

One day, at King Solomon's command, workmen climbed Moriah to build the Holy Temple. By then the splinters and chips of the tablets had become part of a single rock, fused together by time, rain and sun. This rock was used as one of the cornerstones of God's House. Thus, finally, did all the pieces of the broken tablets fulfill their task as the Lord had foretold.